It shouldn't b

She didn't want it

Too dangerous.

"I'm a highly trained US marshal with a decade of experience under my belt. You don't need to worry about me, Ali."

Ali.

Jaxson's voice, the one that had haunted her dreams for a decade. Even when she'd told herself she loved her husband—before she learned his true identity—this man had stolen into her dreams far too often. No matter that the monster she had married had showered her with gifts, no matter that she had bought into the whole fairy-tale life—all of it, every single moment, had been an attempt to erase this man from her heart.

Hadn't worked.

Now here he was, prepared to put his life on the line to protect hers. Or maybe he wanted to see the person she had become. The widow of one of the most sought-after criminals in the country.

A lie.

She had no one to blame but herself.

Now she would be lucky if she survived.

WITNESS PROTECTION WIDOW

USA TODAY Bestselling Author
DEBRA WEBB

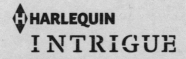

Those employed by the US Marshals Service and the Federal Bureau of Investigation are some of the finest law enforcement folk in our nation. I am in awe of all these dedicated men and women do. As I wrote this story, I took artistic license with certain protocols and operations. After all, romance fiction is about the love story between two people. Everything else is secondary. Enjoy!

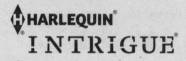

Recycling programs for this product may not exist in your area.

ISBN-13: 978-1-335-13627-5

Witness Protection Widow

Copyright © 2020 by Debra Webb

This edition published by arrangement with Harlequin Books S.A.

For questions and comments about the quality of this book, please contact us at CustomerService@Harlequin.com.

Harlequin Enterprises ULC
22 Adelaide St. West, 40th Floor
Toronto, Ontario M5H 4E3, Canada
www.Harlequin.com

Printed in U.S.A.

Debra Webb is the award-winning *USA TODAY* bestselling author of more than one hundred novels, including those in reader-favorite series Faces of Evil, the Colby Agency and Shades of Death. With more than four million books sold in numerous languages and countries, Debra has a love of storytelling that goes back to her childhood on a farm in Alabama. Visit Debra at www.debrawebb.com.

Books by Debra Webb

Visit the Author Profile page at Harlequin.com.

CAST OF CHARACTERS

Allison James Armone (aka Alice Stewart)—The monster she married is finally dead, murdered by his own father. Allison is determined to see that the Armone family's criminal reign goes down.

US Marshal Jaxson Stevens—Ali James was the love of his life, but they were young and he made a foolish mistake. Now he has the chance to make it right...if he survives keeping her alive.

US Marshal Branch Holloway—He has kept Ali safe for six months, but a car accident puts him out of commission. Was the accident planned by the man who wants Ali dead before she can testify?

Harrison Armone Senior—His family has reigned over organized crime in the Southeast for three generations. His former daughter-in-law is not going to stop him. To him, she is dead already.

Sheriff Colt Tanner—Tanner takes over for Branch until Marshal Stevens arrives. Colt is another of Winchester's local heroes.

Rowan DuPont—Rowan is happy to offer Ali and Jaxson shelter in her home as long as they don't mind sleeping in a funeral home.

Chapter One

Four days until trial

Sunday, February 2
Winchester, Tennessee

It was colder now.

The meteorologist had warned that it might snow on Monday. The temperature was already dropping. She didn't mind. She had no appointments, no deadlines and no place to be—except *here*.

Four days.

Four more days until *the* day.

If she lived that long.

She stopped and surveyed the thick woods around her, making a full three-sixty turn. Nothing but trees and this one trail for as far as the eye could see. The fading sun trickled through the bare limbs. This place had taken her through the last weeks of summer and then fall, and now the end of winter was only weeks away. In all that time, she had only seen one other living human. It was best, they said. For her protection, they insisted.

It was true. But she had never felt more alone in her life. Not since her father died, anyway. That first year after his death, she had to come to terms with being only twenty-four and an orphan. No siblings. No known distant relatives. Just alone.

Bob nudged her. She pushed aside the troubling thoughts and looked down at her black Labrador. "I know, boy. I should get moving. It's cold out here."

She was always keenly aware of the temperature and the time. When it was this cold, the idea of an accidental fall leading to a serious injury haunted her. Other times, when she couldn't bear the walls around her a minute longer, no matter that it was late in the day, she was careful not to stay gone too long. Allowing herself to get caught out in the woods in the dark—no matter that she knew the way back to the cabin by heart—was a bad idea. She started forward once more. Her hiking shoes crunched the rocks and the few frozen leaves scattered across the trail. Bob trotted beside her, his tail wagging happily. She'd never had a dog before coming to this place. When she was growing up, her mother's allergies wouldn't allow pets. Later, when she was out on her own, the apartment building didn't permit pets.

Even after she married and moved into one of Atlanta's megamansions, she couldn't have a dog. Her husband had hated dogs, cats, any sort of pet. How had she not recognized the evil in him then?

Anyone who hated animals so much couldn't be good inside. Whatever good he possessed was only skin-deep and primarily for show.

She hugged herself, rubbed her arms. Thinking of him, even in such simple terms, unsettled her. Soon, she hoped, she would be able to put that part of her life behind her and never look back again.

Never, ever.

"Not soon enough," she muttered.

Most widows grieved the loss of their spouses. She did not. No matter the circumstances, she had never wished him dead, though she had wished many, many times that she had never met him.

But she had met him, and there was no taking back the five years they were married. At first, she had believed the illusion he presented to her. Harrison had been older, very handsome and extremely charming. She had grown up in small-town Georgia on a farm to parents who taught her that fairy tales and dreams weren't real. There was only reality and the lessons that came from hard work and forging forward even when the worst happened. Suddenly, at twenty-six, she was convinced her parents had been wrong. Harrison had swooped into her life like Prince Charming poised to rescue a damsel in distress.

Except she hadn't been in distress, really. But she had been so very hopeful that the future would be bright. Desperately hopeful that good things would one day come her way. Perhaps that was why she didn't see through him for so long. He filled her life with trips to places she'd only dreamed of visiting, like Paris and London. He'd lavished her with gifts: exquisite clothing, endless jewels. Even when she tried to tell him it was too much, more came.

He gave her anything she wanted…except children. He had been married once before and had two college-aged children. Though he was estranged from those adult children, he had no desire to go down that path again. No wish for a chance to have a different outcome. She had been devastated at first. But she had been in love, so she learned to live within that disappointing restriction. Soon after this revelation, she discovered a way to satisfy her mothering needs. She volunteered at Atlanta's rescue mission for at-risk kids. Several months after she began helping out part-time, she was faced with the first unpleasantness about her husband. To her dismay, there were those who believed he and his family were exceptionally bad people.

The shock and horror on the other woman's face when she'd asked, "You're married to Harrison Armone?"

Alice—of course, that wasn't her name then—had smiled, a bit confused, and said, "I am."

The woman had never spoken to her again. In fact, she had done all within her power to avoid her. At least twice she had seen the shocked woman whisper something to another volunteer, who subsequently avoided her, as well. Arriving at the center on her scheduled volunteer days had become something she dreaded rather than looked forward to. From that moment she understood there was something wrong with who she was—the wife of Harrison Armone.

If only she had realized then the level of evil the Armone family represented. Perhaps she would have escaped before the real nightmare that came later. Too bad she hadn't been smart enough to escape before it was too late.

She stared up at the sky, visible only by virtue of the fact that the trees remained bare for the winter. She closed her eyes and tried to force away the images that always followed on the heels of memories even remotely related to him. Those first couple of years had been so blissful. So perfect. For the most part, she had been kept away from the rest of the family. Their estate had been well away from his father's. Her husband went to work each day at a beautiful, upscale building on the most distinguished street in the city. Her life was protected from all things bad and painful.

Until her covolunteer had asked her that damning question.

The worry had grown and swelled inside her like a tidal wave rushing to shore to destroy all in its path. But the trouble didn't begin until a few weeks later. Until she could no longer bear the building pressure inside her.

Her first real mistake was when she asked him—

point-blank—if there was anything he'd failed to disclose before they married.

The question had obviously startled him. He wanted to know where she had gotten such a ridiculous idea. His voice had been calm and kind, as always, tinged with only the tiniest bit of concern. But something about the look in his eyes when he asked the question terrified her. She hadn't wanted to answer his question. He had been far too strangely calm and yet wild-eyed. An unreasonable fear that he would track down her fellow volunteers and give them a hard time had horrified her. After much prodding and far too much pretending at how devastated he was, he had let it go. But she understood that deep down something fundamental had changed.

Whether it was the idea that the bond of trust had been fractured, or that she finally just woke up, she could not look at him the same way again.

The worst part was that he noticed immediately. He realized that thin veil of make-believe had been torn. Every word she uttered, every move she made was suddenly under intense scrutiny. He became suspicious to the point of paranoia. Every day was another in-depth examination of what she had done that day, to whom she had spoken. Then he allowed his true character to show. One by one those ugly family secrets were revealed by his actions. Late-night business meetings that were once handled at his father's house were suddenly held in their home. One night after a particularly long meeting with lots of drinking involved, he confessed that he had wanted to keep the fantasy of their "normal" life, and she had taken it from him.

From that moment forward, she became his prisoner. He punished her in unspeakable ways for taking away his fairy tale.

Now, even with him dead, he still haunted her.

She shook off the memories and focused on the moment. The crisp, clean air. The nature all around her. She'd had her reservations at first, but this place was cleansing for her soul. She had seen so much cruelty and ugliness. This was the perfect sanctuary for healing.

And, of course, hiding.

Only a few more days until the trial. She was the star witness—the first and only witness who had survived to testify against what was left of the Armone family, Harrison Armone Sr. The man had built an empire in the southeast, and Atlanta was his headquarters. The Armone family had run organized crime for three generations—four if you counted her husband, since he would have eventually taken over the business.

But he no longer counted, because he was dead.

Murdered by his own father.

She had witnessed Mr. Armone putting the gun to the back of Harrison's head and pulling the trigger. Then he'd turned to her and announced that she now belonged to him, as did all else his son had hoarded to himself. He would give her adequate grieving time, and then he would expect *things* from her.

Within twenty-four hours, the family's private physician had provided a death certificate, and another family friend with a funeral home had taken care of the rest. No cops were involved, no investigation and certainly no autopsy. Cause of death was listed as a heart attack. The obituary was pompous and filled half a page in the *Atlanta Journal-Constitution*.

It wasn't until three days after the funeral that she had her first opportunity to attempt an escape.

She had prepared well. For months before Harrison's death she had been readying for an opportunity to flee. She had hidden away a considerable amount of cash and numerous prepaid cards that could not be traced back to her. She'd even purchased a phone— one for which minutes could be bought at the supermarket. When the day came, she left the house with nothing more than the clothes on her back. The money and cards were tucked into her jacket. The entire jacket was basically padded with cash and plastic beneath the layer of fabric that served as the lining. She'd worn her favorite running shoes and workout clothes.

This was another way she had prepared. Shortly after her husband had started to show his true colors, she had become obsessed with fitness and building her physical strength.

The week before her own personal D-day, she had gone to the gym and stashed jeans, a sweatshirt, a ball cap, big sunglasses and a clasp for pinning her long blond hair out of sight beneath the cap in a locker.

When D-day arrived, she had left the gym through a rear exit and jogged the nearly three miles to the Four Seasons, where she'd taken a taxi to the bus station. She'd loaded onto the bus headed to Birmingham, Alabama. In Birmingham, she had boarded another bus to Nashville, Tennessee, and finally from Nashville to Louisville, Kentucky. Each time she changed something about her appearance. She picked up another jacket or traded with another traveler. Changed the hat and the way she wore her hair. Eventually she reached her destination. Scared to death but with no other recourse, she walked into the FBI office and told whoever would listen her story.

Now she was here.

The small clearing where her temporary home— a rustic cabin—stood came into view. The setting sun spilled the last of its glow across the mountain.

In the middle of nowhere, on a mountain, she awaited the moment when she would tell the world what kind of monster Harrison Armone Sr. was. His son had been equally evil, but no one deserved to be murdered, particularly by his own father.

Those last three years of their marriage, when he'd recognized that she knew what he was, his decision to permit her to see and hear things had somehow been calculated. She supposed he had hoped to keep her scared into submission. She had been scared, all right. Scared to death. But she had planned her escape when no one was looking.

The FBI had been thrilled with what she had to offer. But they had also recognized that keeping her alive until and through the trial wouldn't be easy. Welcome to witness protection. She had been moved once already. The security of the first location where she'd been hidden away had been breached after only three months. She'd had no idea anything was going on when two marshals had shown up to take her away.

So far things had gone smoothly in Winchester. She kept to herself. Ordered her food online and the marshal assigned to her picked up the goods and delivered the load to her. Though she had a small SUV for emergencies, she did not leave the property and put herself in a position where someone might see and remember her.

Anything she needed, the marshal took care of.

The SUV parked next to the house was equipped with all-wheel drive since she lived out in the woods on a curvy mountain road. US Marshal Branch Holloway checked on her regularly. She had a special phone for emergencies and for contacting him. He'd made her feel at ease from the beginning. He was patient and kind. Far more understanding than the first marshal assigned to her had been.

For this she was immensely grateful.

Yes. She had married an evil man. Yes. She had been a fool. But she hadn't set out to do so. She had been taught to believe the best in everyone until she had reason to see otherwise.

Two years. Yes, it had taken a long time to see past the seemingly perfect facade he had built for her, but she was only human. She had loved him. She had waited a very long time to feel that way again after her first heartbreak at the age of twenty-one.

"Get over it," she muttered to herself. Beating herself up for being naive wasn't going to change history.

This—she surveyed the bare trees and little cabin— was her life now. At least until the trial.

In the movies witness protection was made to look like a glamourous adventure, but that could not be farther from the truth. It was terrifying. Justice depended on her survival to testify in court, and her survival depended upon the marshal assigned to her case and on her own actions. The FBI had shown her how much bigger this case was than just the murder of her husband and the small amount of knowledge she had absorbed. The Armones had murdered countless people. Drugs, guns and all sorts of other criminal activities were a part of their network. She alone held the power to end the Armone reign.

No matter that the family was so obviously evil, she still couldn't understand how a father could murder his son—his only child. Of course, it was Harrison's own fault. He had been secretly working to overthrow his father. The old man was nearing seventy and had no plans to retire. Harrison had wanted to be king.

Instead, he'd gotten dead.

She shuddered at the idea that his father—after murdering him—had intended to take his widow as his own plaything.

Sick. The man was absolutely disgusting. Like his son, he was a charming and quite handsome man for his age. But beneath the surface lived a monster.

Once the trial was over, she hoped she never had to think of him again, much less see him.

Staying alert to her surroundings, she unlocked the back door and sent Bob inside ahead of her. He was trained to spot trouble. She wasn't overly concerned at this point. If anything had been amiss, he would have warned her as they approached the cabin.

The dogs were a new addition to the witness protection family. She hadn't had a dog at the first location. It wasn't until she'd arrived here and had Bob living with her that she'd realized how very lonely she had been for a very long time. Since well before her husband was murdered.

She locked the door behind her, taking care to check all the locks. Then she followed Bob through the three rooms. There was a small living-dining-kitchen combination, a bedroom with an attached bath and the mudroom–laundry room at the back. Furnishings were sparse, but she had what she needed.

Since cell service was sketchy at best, she had a state-of-the-art signal booster. She had a generator in case the power went out and a bug-out bag if it became necessary to cut and run.

She shivered. The fire had gone out. She kept on her jacket while she added logs to the fireplace and kindling to get it started. Within a couple of minutes, the fire was going. She'd had a fireplace as a kid, so relearning her way around this one hadn't been so bad. She went back to the kitchen and turned on the kettle for tea.

Bob growled low in his throat and stared toward the front door.

She froze. Her phone was in her hip pocket. Her gun was still in her waistband at the small of her back. This was something else Marshal Holloway had insisted upon. He'd taught her how to use a handgun. They'd held many target practices right behind this cabin.

A creak beyond the front door warned that someone was on the porch. She eased across the room and went to the special peephole that had been installed. There was one on each side of the cabin, allowing for views all the way around. A man stood on the porch. He was the typical local cowboy. Jeans and boots. Hat in his hands. Big truck in the drive. Just like Marshal Holloway.

But she did not know this man.

"Alice Stewart, if you're in there, it's okay for you to open the door. I'm Sheriff Colt Tanner. Branch sent me."

Her heart thudding, she held perfectly still. Branch would never send someone to her without letting her know first. If for some reason he couldn't tell her in advance, they had a protocol for these situations.

She reached back, fingers curled about the butt of her weapon. Bob moved stealthily toward the door.

"I know you're concerned about opening the door to a stranger, but you need to trust me. Branch has been in an accident, and he's in the hospital undergoing surgery right now. No matter that his injuries were serious, he refused to go into surgery until he spoke to me and I assured him I would look after you, ma'am."

Worry joined the mixture of fear and dread churning inside her. She hoped Branch wasn't hurt too badly. He had a wife and a daughter.

She opened her mouth to ask about his condition, but then she snapped it shut. The man at her door had not said the code word.

"Wait," he said. "I know what the problem is. I forgot to say 'superhero.' He told me that's your code word."

Relief rushed through her. She moved to the door and unlocked the four dead bolts, then opened it. When she faced the man—Sheriff Tanner—she asked, "Is he going to be okay?"

The sheriff ducked his head. "I sure hope so. Branch is a good friend of mine. May I come in?"

"Quiet, Bob," she ordered the dog at her side as she backed up and allowed the sheriff to come inside before closing the door. She resisted the impulse to lock it and leaned against it instead. Holloway wouldn't have trusted this man if he wasn't one of the good guys.

Still, standing here with a stranger after all these months, she couldn't help feeling a little uneasy. Bob sat at her feet, his gaze tracking every move the stranger made.

"Is there anything you need, ma'am? Anything at all. I'll be happy to bring you any supplies or just…" He shrugged. "Whatever you need."

The kettle screamed out, making her jump. She'd completely forgotten about it. "I'll be right back."

She hurried to the kitchen and turned off the flame beneath the whistling kettle. She took a breath, pushed her hair behind her ears and walked back into the living room.

"Thank you for coming, Sheriff, but I have everything I need."

"All right." He pulled a card from his shirt pocket and offered it to her. "Call me if you need anything. I'll check on you again later today and give you an update on Branch's condition."

She studied the card. "Thank you." She looked up at him then. "I appreciate your concern. Please let the marshal know I'm hoping for his speedy recovery."

"Will do." He gave her another of those quick nods. "I'll be on my way then."

Before she opened the door for him to go, she had to ask. "Are his injuries life-threatening?"

"He was real lucky, ma'am. Things could have been far worse. Thankfully, he's stable, and we have every reason to believe he'll be fine."

"What about his wife?"

"She wasn't with him, so she's fine. She's at the

hospital waiting for him to come out of surgery. If you're certain you don't need me for anything, I'm going back there now."

"Really, I'm fine. Thank you."

When the sheriff had said his goodbyes and headed out to his truck, she locked the door—all four dead bolts. She watched as the truck turned around and rolled away. She told herself that Marshal Holloway's accident most likely didn't have anything to do with her or the trial. Still, she couldn't help but worry just a little.

What if they had found her? What if hurting the marshal was just the first step in getting to her? Old man Armone was pure evil. He would want her to know in advance that he was coming just to be sure she felt as much fear as possible. Instilling fear gave him great pleasure.

Harrison Armone Sr. had a small army at his beck and call. All were trained mercenaries. Ruthless, like him. Proficient in killing. Relentless in attaining their target. They would be hunting her. If being careful would get her through this, she had nothing to worry about. But that alone would never be enough. She needed help and luck on her side.

With this unexpected development, she would need to be extra vigilant.

"Bob."

He looked up at her expectantly.

"We have to be especially alert, my friend."

The devil might be coming.

And he wouldn't be alone.

Chapter Two

Winchester Hospital

Jaxson Stevens left Nashville as soon as he heard the news of the accident. He and Branch Holloway had been assigned together briefly before Holloway transferred back to his hometown of Winchester. Holloway was a good guy and a damned fine marshal. Jax was more than happy to back him up until he was on his feet again.

He parked his SUV in the lot and headed for the hospital entrance. He hadn't been in the Winchester area in ages. He hailed from the Pacific Northwest, and he'd taken an assignment in Seattle when he completed training with the marshal service. He had ended up spending the better part of the first decade of his career on that side of the country. Then he'd needed a change. He'd landed in Nashville last year.

Truth is, he'd hadn't exactly wanted to spend time in the southeast, but it was a necessary step in his career ladder. There was a woman he'd met when he was in training at Glynco. The two of them had a very intense few months together, and he'd wondered about her for years after moving to Seattle. They'd both been so young when they first met. He'd kept an eye on her for years while she finished college, certain they would end up together again at some point. He'd anonymously helped out when her father passed away.

Then his notions of a romantic reunion had come to a grinding halt after she moved to Atlanta.

She had gotten married. He shook his head. All those years, she had haunted his dreams. He'd thought he had known her, thought they had something that deserved a second go when the time was right. He'd definitely never felt that connection with anyone else.

But he had been wrong. Dead wrong.

A woman who would marry a man like she had was not someone he knew at all. He imagined she fully comprehended what the world thought of her choice about now.

Irrelevant, he reminded himself. The past was the past. Nothing he could do about the years he wasted wondering about her. He was happy in Nashville for now. He had just turned thirty-two, and he had big career plans. There was plenty of time to get serious about a personal relationship. God knew his parents and his sister constantly nagged him about his single status.

Maybe after this case was buttoned up. The witness had to be at trial on Thursday. After that, he was taking a vacation and making some personal decisions. Maybe it was time he took inventory of his life rather than just pouring everything into the job.

The hospital had that disinfectant smell that lingered in every single hospital he'd ever stepped into. The odor triggered unpleasant memories he'd just as soon not revisit in this lifetime. Losing his younger brother was hard as a ten-year-old. He couldn't imagine what his parents had suffered.

His mom warned him often that he shouldn't allow that loss to get in the way of having a family. He had never really considered that he chose not to get too serious about a relationship because of what happened when he was a kid, but maybe he had. His parents had spent better than twenty years telling him that what happened wasn't his fault. Didn't matter. He would always believe it was. He should have been watching more closely. He should never have allowed his little brother so close to the water's edge.

He should have been better prepared to help him if something went wrong.

Why the hell had he gone down that road?

Jax shook his head and strode across the lobby, kicking the past back to where it belonged—behind him. A quick check with the information desk and he was on his way to the third floor. He followed the signs to Holloway's room.

His gaze came to rest on his old friend, and he grimaced. The left side of the man's face was bruised and swollen as if he'd slugged it out and lost big-time. What he could see of Holloway's left shoulder was bruised, as well. "You look like hell, buddy."

Branch Holloway opened his eyes. "Pretty much feel like it, too. Glad you could make it, Stevens."

Jax moved to the side of his bed. "What happened? You tick off the wrong cowboy?"

Tennessee was full of cowboys. Jax had tried a pair of boots. Not for him. And the hat—well, that just wasn't his style. He was more a city kind of guy. Jeans, pullovers and a good pair of hiking shoes and he was good to go. He was, however, rather fond of leather. He'd had the leather jacket he wore for over a decade.

"I wish I could tell you a heroic story of chasing bad guys and surviving a shootout, but it was nothing like that. A deer decided my truck was in his way. I didn't hit him, but I did hit the ditch and then a couple of trees. One tree in particular tried real hard to do me in."

Jax made a face. "Sounds like you're damned lucky."

"That's what they say, but I gotta tell you right now I'm not feeling too lucky. My wife says I will when I see my truck. It's totaled."

"Can I get you anything?" Jax glanced at the water pitcher on the bedside table.

"No, thanks. My wife was here until just a few minutes ago. She's hovered over me since the paramedics brought me in. Between her and the nurses, I'm good, trust me."

Jax nodded. "You didn't want to discuss the case by phone. I take it this is a dark one." Some cases were listed as dark. These were generally the ones where the person or persons who wanted to hurt the witness had an abundance of resources, making the witness far more vulnerable. Sometimes a case was dark simply because of the priority tag associated with the investigation. The least number of people possible were involved with dark cases.

There were bad guys in this world, and then there were *really* bad guys.

"Need-to-know basis only," Holloway said. "We're only days out from trial. Keeping this witness safe is essential. At this point, we pretty much need to keep her under surveillance twenty-four hours a day until trial. This couldn't have happened at a worse time."

"Understandable," Jax agreed.

"I'm sure you're familiar with the Armone case. It's been all over the news."

Jax's eyebrows went up with a jolt of surprise. "That's not a name I expected to hear. I knew the patriarch of the family was awaiting trial, but I haven't kept up with the details. Besides, that's a ways out of our district."

"The powers that be felt moving her out of Georgia until trial would help keep her safe. They've kept the details quiet on this one to the greatest extent possible. Even with all those precautions and a media blackout, her first location was jeopardized."

Her? A bad, bad feeling began a slow creep through Jax.

"Hell of a time for you to be out of commission," he said instead of demanding who the hell the witness was. *This* could not happen. Maybe it was someone else. A secretary or other associate of the old man. Or maybe of the son, since he was dead. His death may have prompted someone—an illicit lover, perhaps—to come forward.

"Tell me about it," Holloway grumbled.

"Why don't you bring me up to speed," Jax suggested. "We'll go from there."

"The file's under my pillow."

Jax chuckled as he reached beneath the thin hospital pillow. "I have to say, this is going the distance for the job."

"We do what we have to, right?"

"Right." Jax opened the file, his gaze landing on the attached photo. He blinked. Looked again. She looked exactly as she had ten years ago.

"You okay there?" Holloway asked. "You look like you just saw a ghost."

"Full disclosure, Holloway." Jax frowned. "I know this woman." No. That was wrong. He didn't just know this woman—he knew her intimately. Had been disappointed in and angry with her for years now.

"Well, hell. If this is a problem, we should call

someone else in as quickly as possible. I've got the local sheriff, a friend of mine, taking care of things now. But I can't keep him tied up this way. No one wants this bastard to get away this time. We've got him. As long as she lives to testify, he's not walking."

Holloway was right. The Armone family had escaped justice far too long. "I've got this." Jax cleared his head. If Holloway thought he was not up to par, he would insist on calling in someone else. Jax was startled, no denying it. But he wanted to do this. He had to do this. For reasons that went beyond the job. Purely selfish reasons. "You can count on me. I just wanted to be up front. We knew each other a long time ago."

"If you're sure," Holloway countered. "I'm confident I can count on you. I just don't want to put you in an unnecessarily awkward situation. Sometimes the past can adversely affect the present."

Jax felt his gut tighten. Maybe he wasn't as ready for this as he'd thought.

No choice.

If he didn't do this, he would never fully extract her from his head.

The what-ifs would haunt him forever.

"I can handle it. Like I said, we haven't seen each other in years," he assured the other man. "No one wants this family to go down more than me."

That part was more true than he cared to admit.

"If we're lucky, that family will be history when this trial is done," Holloway said. "The son is dead.

Now all we need is for the father to be put away for the rest of his sorry life." Holloway searched his face as if looking for any uncertainty. "I can ask Sheriff Tanner to show you the way to her location if you're sure we're good to go."

"That works."

"Thanks, Stevens. I'll owe you one."

THE CABIN WAS well out of town. Sheriff Colt Tanner had met Jax at the courthouse and led the way. Tanner had last checked on the witness an hour ago. At this stage, Jax wasn't going to simply check on her—he was to stick with her until she walked into that courtroom to testify. Protect, transport…whatever necessary.

On the drive to her location, he had decided he really didn't have a problem with doing the job. He couldn't deny that he had spent a great deal of time trying to find Allison James, aka Alice Stewart, the widow of Harrison Armone Jr., illegal drugs and weapons kingpin of the southeast. In fact, he wanted to do this. He wanted to learn what had happened to the sweet young woman he had known during his training. How had the shy, soft-spoken girl become the wife of one of the most wanted bastards on the minds of FBI, ATF and DEA agents alike? Maybe it was sheer curiosity, but he needed to understand how the hell that happened.

The actual problem, in his opinion, was how she would feel about him being the one charged with her safety. She no doubt would understand that he was well aware of who she had gotten involved with and would be disgusted by it. Members of law enforcement from Atlanta to DC had wished for a way to eradicate this problem.

He guessed he would find out soon enough.

Jax parked his SUV next to hers and got out. She was likely watching out the window. Tanner had updated her on Holloway's condition and told her that a new marshal would be arriving shortly. Jax had no idea whether the sheriff had given her his name. If he had, she might be waiting behind that door with her weapon drawn. Not that she had any reason to be holding a grudge. He'd asked her to go with him to Seattle, but she had turned him down. No matter that he shouldn't—didn't want to—he wondered if she had attempted to track him down at any time during those early years after he left and before she made the mistake of her life.

Had she even thought of him?

He hadn't asked her to marry him, but they had talked about marriage. They had talked about the future and what they each wanted. She'd had expectations. He had recognized this. But that hadn't stopped him from leaving when an opportunity he couldn't turn down came his way. She wouldn't go. Her father was still alive and alone. She didn't want to move so far away from him. What was he supposed to do? Ignore the offer he had hoped for from the day he decided to join the marshal service?

That little voice that warned when he had crossed the line shouted at him now. He had been selfish. No question. But he'd had family, too, and they had been on the West Coast. An unwinnable situation.

He walked up to the porch. Climbed the steps and crossed to the door. Aware she was certainly watching, he raised his fist and knocked.

She didn't say a word or make a sound, but he felt her on the other side of the door. Only inches from him. He closed his eyes and recalled her scent. Soft, subtle. She always smelled like citrus. Never wore makeup. She had the most beautiful blue eyes he had ever seen.

The door opened and she stood there, looking exactly the way she had ten years ago—no makeup, no fussy hairdo, just Ali. The big black Lab the sheriff had told him about stood next to her.

For one long moment, she stared at him and he stared at her.

He inhaled a deep breath, acknowledged the scent of her—the scent he would have recognized anywhere.

"Say it."

For a moment he felt confused at her statement.

"Say it," she repeated. "I'm not letting you inside until you do."

He understood then. "Superhero."

She stepped back, and he walked in. The door closed behind him, locks tumbling into place. The dog sniffed him, eying him suspiciously.

She scratched the Lab's head, and the dog settled down. "No one told me you were the one coming."

She stood close to the wall on his left, beyond arm's reach. Now that he had a chance to really look, she was thinner than before. Fear glittered in her eyes. Beyond the fear was something else. A weariness. Sadness, too, he concluded.

"I didn't know it was you until I arrived in Winchester." He held her gaze, refused to let her off the hook. He didn't want this to be easy. Appreciating her discomfort was low. He knew this, and still he couldn't help it. "I'm glad I'm the one Holloway called. I want to help. If that's okay with you."

"I'm certain Marshal Holloway wouldn't have called you if you weren't up to the task." She shrugged. "As for the past, it was a long time ago. It's hardly relevant now."

She was right. It had been a long time. Still, the idea that she played it off so nonchalantly didn't sit so well. No need for her to know the resentment or whatever the hell it was he harbored related to her decisions or the whirlwind of emotions she had set reeling inside him now. This was work. Business. The job. It wasn't personal.

He hitched a thumb toward the door. "I picked up a pizza. It's a little early for lunch, but I was on the road damned early this morning."

"Make yourself at home. You don't need my permission to eat."

No, he did not. "I'll grab my bag and the pizza."

He walked out to his SUV. He took a breath. Struggled to slow his heart rate. He had an assignment to complete, and it was essential he pulled his head out of the past and focused on the present. What happened ten years ago or five years ago was irrelevant. What mattered was now. Keeping her safe. Getting her in that courtroom to put a scumbag away.

He grabbed his bag and the pizza and headed back to the cabin. She opened the door for him and then locked the four dead bolts. He placed the pizza on the table and dropped his bag by the sofa. He imagined that would be his bed for the foreseeable future. The place didn't look large enough to have two bedrooms.

"This is Bob, by the way," she said of the dog who stayed at her side.

He nodded. "Nice to meet you, Bob."

Bob stared at him with a healthy dose of either skepticism or continued suspicion.

"Would you like water or a cola?"

Since beer was out of the question, he went for a cola. She walked to the fridge and grabbed two. On the way to the table, she snagged the roll of paper towels from the counter and brought that along, as well. She sat down directly across the table. Apparently she had decided to join him. He passed her a slice, grabbed one of his own and then dug in. Eating would prevent the need for conversation. If he chewed slowly enough, he could drag this out for a while.

She sipped her drink. "You finally get married?"

He was surprised she asked. Left her open for his questions. And he really wanted a number of answers from her. At the moment dealing with all the emotions and sensations related to just being in the same room with her was all he could handle.

"No. Never engaged. Never married."

Silence dragged on for another minute or so while they ate. Keeping his attention away from her lips as she ate proved more difficult than he'd expected. Frankly, he was grateful when she polished off the last bit.

"Technically," she pointed out as she reached for a second slice, "*we* were engaged—informally."

He went still, startled that his heart didn't do the same. He hadn't expected her to bring that up under the circumstances. *"Technically,"* he repeated, "I suppose you're right."

"How long were you in Seattle?"

"Until last year." He wiped his hands on a napkin. "I'm sorry about your father."

"It was a tough time."

"Yeah, I'm sure it was." He had come so close to attending the funeral, but he had wondered if he would be welcome, so he hadn't.

He bit into his pizza to prevent asking if that was why she'd ran into the arms of a criminal. Had she wanted someone to take care of her? A sugar daddy or whatever? Fury lit inside him. He forced the thoughts away. It didn't matter that they had spent months intensely focused on each other, practically inseparable. That had been a long time ago. What-ever they had then was long gone by the time she married Armone. All this emotion was unnecessary. Pointless. Frustrating as hell, actually.

"What about your parents?" She dabbed at her lips with a napkin. "Your sister?"

"The parents are doing great. Talking about buy-ing a winter home in Florida. Is that cliché or what?" He managed a smile, hoped to lighten the situation.

She looked completely at ease. Calm. Maybe he was the only one having trouble.

Her lips lifted into a small smile. "A little."

"My sister is married with three kids." He shook his head. "I don't know how she does it."

"She's lucky."

"You have kids?" He knew the answer, but he didn't know the reason.

"No. *He* didn't want children. He had two with his first wife." She stared at the pizza box for a mo-ment. "Looking back, I was very fortunate he didn't."

For now, he guided the conversation away from the bastard she'd married. He asked another question to which he already knew the answer. "You were de-termined to finish school. Did you manage?"

"I did. With taking care of my father it took for-ever, but I finally got it done."

"That's great."

More of that suffocating silence. He stared at the pizza, suddenly having no appetite.

"Your career is going well?" she asked.

"It is. The work is challenging and fulfilling."

She stood. "Thank you for the pizza."

He watched as she carried her napkin and cola can to the trash. She stood at the sink and stared out the window.

The urge to demand how she could have married a man like Harrison Armone burned on his tongue, but he swallowed it back.

"I think maybe they should send someone else."

Her words surprised him. Flustered him. He stood, the legs of his chair scraping across the wood floor. "Why? I see no reason we can't put the past behind us."

She turned to face him but stayed right where she was, her fingers gripping the edge of the countertop as if she feared gravity would fail her. "If *he* finds me, he will kill me. If you're in the way, he'll kill you, too."

Chapter Three

The man she had fallen head over heels in love with when she was barely twenty-one stared at her as if she'd confessed to the world's most heinous crime. How could he be the one they sent to protect her?

It shouldn't be him.

She didn't want it to be him.

Too dangerous.

"I'm a highly trained US marshal with a decade of experience under my belt. You don't need to worry about me, Ali."

Ali. Her throat tightened as she attempted to swallow. His voice, the one that had haunted her dreams for a decade. Even when she'd told herself she loved her husband—before she learned his true identity— this man had stolen into her dreams far too often. No matter that the monster she had married had showered her with gifts, no matter that she had bought into the whole fairy-tale life…all of it, every single moment, had been an attempt to erase this man from her heart.

Hadn't worked.

Now, here he was, prepared to put his life on the line to protect hers. Or maybe he wanted to see the person she had become. The widow of one of the most sought-after criminals in the country.

A lie.

Her entire existence these past five years had been a lie.

She had no one to blame but herself. She had allowed herself to buy completely into the fantasy.

Now she would be lucky if she survived.

"Why?" she demanded.

His gaze narrowed—those brown eyes that made her shiver with just a look. "Why what?"

"Why you? There's what, a couple thousand marshals? Why you?" she repeated.

"Holloway and I worked together in Nashville for a while before he relocated to Winchester. When he had his accident, he reached out to me. There wasn't time to go through the usual red tape. He needed someone with you ASAP. So here I am."

She shook her head. "This doesn't work for me."

She surely had some choice in the matter. After all, she was the witness—the *star* witness, according to the prosecutor. Without her, their case would fall apart at the hands of the dozen or so powerful attorneys Armone kept on retainer.

Jax shrugged. "I can pass along your objection to the powers that be. It's possible someone else could take over for me, but that would take time, and time is short. The trial is in four days. We don't want to do anything that might draw attention to where you are."

No. This would not work. She couldn't be this close to him. Night and day in such a cramped space. Impossible. More important, she did not want him to get hurt. "Call them. See what they can do."

He took a step toward her. Then another. She told herself to breathe, but her lungs refused the order.

"Is there some reason you don't trust me? Maybe you believe I'm not capable of handling the job?"

"I have no idea what your credentials are," she improvised. "I'm just not comfortable like this… with you."

He nodded once. "I see. You don't like being alone with me?" Another step disappeared between them.

Her heart refused to stop its pounding. She stared at him and told the truth. The truth was all she had left. "In light of the circumstances, I would like to be reasonable, but I'm having some difficulty. Yes."

For a moment he hesitated, then he said, "I'll stay out of your personal space. You have my word."

He backed away, turned and crossed to the other side of the room, and sat down on the sofa.

When she could breathe again, she dragged in a lungful of much-needed air. "I usually take a walk at this time every afternoon."

It wasn't necessary for him to know she'd already taken a walk this morning. Sometimes she took a couple of walks in a day in addition to a nice long run. Right now, she needed out of this too-tight space. She needed to breathe. To think.

"All right." He stood. "I'll go with you."

Well, that didn't work out the way she'd planned. "I usually go alone. With Bob, of course."

"Starting today, you don't go anywhere alone."

No point arguing the decree. He likely had been briefed on things she was not privy to as of yet. She understood there were aspects of the case she shouldn't or couldn't know. At first she hadn't been happy about that part. Eventually she had come to terms with focusing on her role and allowing the marshal and the prosecutor to do what they needed to do.

Frankly, it wasn't that different from her life with Harrison. He had told her what to do and when to do it. The funny thing was, she hadn't realized how controlling he was at first. In the beginning, their life together had felt as if he were pampering her and taking exquisite care of her. Her entire adult life had been about taking care of others. First her mother and then her father. Not that she had minded. She had done what any daughter would do. College had been more of the same. Go to class, do the work. Since she'd had to squeeze college in around the health issues of her parents, she had been twenty-five when she finally attained her undergraduate degree. Then she'd moved to Atlanta and met Harrison, and everything had changed.

Suddenly someone was taking care of her. Mak-

ing the decisions. Showing her the world and show-
ering her with luxurious gifts.

It was hard to believe now that she hadn't recognized her fairy-tale life was too good to be true.

The trouble was, she had needed it to be true.
Sometimes a need was so powerful that it overrode
good sense.

She had thrown good sense and logic out the window.

Beating herself up about it more wasn't going to
change the facts. She'd done what she'd done, and
now she was in the middle of this situation.

"Let's go, Bob." She patted her thigh, and he
jumped up to follow her.

She locked up and handed Jax the key she typically kept in her pocket. If he was in charge, she
might as well turn that over to him, as well.

The sun hovered near the treetops as they walked
away from the cabin. She surveyed the blue sky.
It was supposed to snow late tonight or tomorrow.
Snow would be nice. A dusting or two had happened since she arrived in this location. A whole
two inches had fallen on Christmas Eve night. She
had needed that beautiful display of nature. She'd
felt so intensely alone.

Christmas afternoon Marshal Holloway had
shown up with a veritable buffet of goodies. His wife
and mother had made a lovely Christmas lunch, and
they had wanted to share with her. He'd also brought
a little decorated tree. The sort you picked up at the

grocery store. Those simple gestures had touched her so deeply. That was the moment when she realized she might actually be okay eventually.

If she survived beyond the trial, she could make a new life. There were still plenty of good people in this world. She would be fine.

If she survived.

"What's your plan for when this is over?"

The sound of his voice, the deep rumble that had whispered in her dreams for so long, made her pulse flutter.

"I really haven't thought that far ahead. Mostly I'm focused on surviving."

"I'm sure you've met with the AUSA in your case and done the necessary prepping."

Assistant US Attorney Samuel Keller was the federal prosecutor in the case against the Armone family. Ali had met with him twice. An attorney had been assigned to represent her interests, and she'd met with him the same. The situation was fairly cut-and-dried. She had never been involved with the family business. She had only in the past two years started to learn and document information she intended to one day take to the FBI.

"Yes. His name is Keller. Samuel Keller."

Jax nodded. "I'm familiar with Keller. He has a high conviction rate, and he's ambitious. Two important assets for the case."

Ali hadn't liked him very much. He'd made her feel cheap during their first meeting. When they'd met the second time, he had been far kinder. Perhaps someone above him had warned that he shouldn't frustrate or anger their star witness.

"I don't think he's a very nice man," she admitted. Not that she could trust her instincts as well as she'd once believed. They had steered her wrong with Harrison. Dead wrong.

"Being nice isn't necessarily a good thing when it comes to prosecutors. Ruthlessness and fearlessness are far more attractive in their line of work."

The notion made some sort of sense, she supposed. "I guess so."

Bob galloped ahead, spotting a bird or a squirrel. A gust of chilly wind whipped through the trees. She shivered, despite the sweatshirt she wore.

"When did you move to Atlanta?"

She studied his profile a moment, noting the little differences. A laugh line or two around the eyes. Slightly more angular jaw. He was leaner. "I finished my last semester of college, and I just couldn't see going back home to that empty house. Mom and Dad were both gone. I needed a fresh start. Something new. A challenge." She shrugged. "I was offered a position with an up-and-coming company. It felt right, so I threw caution to the wind."

More so than she intended.

"Did you sell the farm?"

He had been to her parents' farm once. It wasn't anything to brag about. A rambling old house on a hundred acres. She had loved the barn and the big old oak trees best of all. She'd lived there her whole life except for when she was away at college and then had moved to Atlanta afterward.

"I did. It was a difficult decision, but I couldn't stay. There were no career opportunities in the area, and I was reasonably certain that farming wasn't my strong suit. I was pleased that a guy who attended high school with me had just gotten married and wanted to buy the place. He and his wife have two kids now. They've fixed up the house and are really making a go of the farming gig. My dad would be happy."

Silence settled for a long while. The sun was dropping, leaving the sky streaked with faded grays and blues. The temperature was dropping, too. She should have grabbed her jacket. But she had been thinking of only one thing—getting out of that tiny cabin.

"Does your father still build boats?"

Ali had met his parents twice. Once when they came to Georgia to visit him and once for Thanksgiving when she and Jax flew out to visit them. They lived near the water, and boating was his father's love—second only to his family. He was one of the few people who still built fishing boats by hand. The craftsmanship was utterly amazing. Despite the gray hair, it had been easy to see that Jax had inherited his good looks from his father. His mother was a schoolteacher and a very lovely woman. She and Ali had quickly connected. Ali's mother had died the year before, and she had desperately needed that bond.

"He is. I can't see him ever stopping. He loves it too much."

Ali appreciated that level of passion. "What about your mother? Is she still teaching?"

"She is, but not in the classroom. She's the middle school principal now." He chuckled. "I'm just glad that didn't happen when I was in school. It was bad enough knowing she was in the same wing teaching biology during eighth grade."

Ali smiled. "She insisted you were a really good student."

"She only told you that because she liked you and didn't want to scare you off." He glanced at her. "I was a bit of a class clown."

Ali looked away. She watched as Bob sniffed at the undergrowth farther up the path. She wondered if she would be able to keep Bob when this was over. She couldn't imagine life without him. They'd been together for six months. The same amount of time she and Jax had spent together a decade ago.

Ali picked up her pace. It was getting colder, and the sun would set soon. They should probably turn back at the top of the next rise. As they reached it, she called Bob to come and waited for him to reach her side. Then they started down together, Jax trailing after.

The idea that he would be sleeping on the sofa no more than thirty feet away needled at the back of her mind. She didn't want to be that close to him in the darkness.

Too late to do anything about that now.

BY THE TIME the clearing came into view, it was dark and the occasional snowflake floated down in front of them.

Bob abruptly froze. A growl sounded low in his throat.

"What's the matter, boy?" Ali surveyed the area as she spoke.

Jax suddenly pulled her into the tree line. "Someone's at the house."

The whispered words no sooner brushed against her ear than she spotted the man peering into the house via the back door. He looked for a moment and then moved to a window. He tried the sash to see if it would move. It didn't. She kept the windows locked. Then he moved around the corner of the house.

"Take Bob and disappear deeper into these trees," Jax whispered with a nod to his left.

She nodded and did as he'd told her, ushering Bob along when he wanted to stop and stare and growl. Thank God he didn't bark. She crouched down between two trees and watched the clearing. Bob sat next to her, his warm body reassuring.

The quiet was deafening. She stretched her neck in an attempt to see Jax. It was too dark to see well. She could see the cabin because she'd left the lights on. The moonlight lit up the area around it the slightest little bit. She tried not to blink for fear she'd miss Jax or the other man.

Shouted voices echoed in the night. She strained to see.

Wherever they were, it wasn't on the back side of the cabin.

More angry voices. Then only one.

Jax.

She pushed out of her crouch and started forward. Bob stayed right on her heels. She moved closer to the clearing, careful to stay in the tree line. Jax had the man pushed against the cabin, his weapon boring into his skull.

Was this someone Armone had sent?

She eased closer still.

Jax repeated his demand to know the man's name. Finally he sputtered, "Teddy Scott. I work for the utility company. There was a call about the service out here. I came to check it out."

"On Sunday?" Jax asked, his skepticism clear.

"Hey, man, I just do what I'm told. I work nights, days, weekends. Whenever the call comes."

Except no one had called. Not from this address.

She dared to slip from the tree line. The guy's gaze strayed to her. Jax jerked his errant attention back to him.

"Everything okay?" she called out to Jax.

"Maybe," he said. "Maybe not. Go out to my car and grab the handcuffs from the console, would you?"

Ali hurried around to the front of the cabin. She

went to his SUV and opened the passenger side door. She leaned over the seat and opened the console. She reached in and grabbed the metal cuffs.

She rushed back to where he held the man and handed him the cuffs.

"Turn around," he ordered the interloper.

The man turned around. "Seriously, if you'll just call the utility company, you'll learn I'm telling the truth. The call came in, and I came out."

"I'm not saying I don't believe you, Mr. Scott." Jax snapped one cuff onto the man's right wrist and one onto the metal pole attached to the cabin. "The problem is, I have to be sure."

Needing someplace to look besides at the man who may have been sent to find her, Ali traced the path of the pole. It went up to the roof. *Antennae.* As many times as she'd walked that path beyond the cabin, she hadn't paid the slightest attention to the antennae. It was just a part of the house.

And now it was the part that would keep Mr. Scott right here until Jax figured out exactly who he was or what to do about him. He withdrew the man's wallet and checked his ID, she presumed. He carried no weapon, which seemed odd for one of Armone's thugs.

Jax started toward her. She braced herself for his touch as he reached for her. His fingers wrapped around her upper arm. "Get your purse, if you carry one, and let's go for a ride. I'll call Sheriff Tanner and let him get to the bottom of this."

Ali hurried inside and grabbed her cross-body bag. She tucked the emergency cell phone inside. "Come," she said to Bob.

Her faithful friend followed her to the front, where Jax waited. He was on his cell phone, presumably with Tanner. He provided the man's description and the name he listed on his ID, which was the same one he'd given. Jax listened for a bit and then ended the call.

"Is Tanner coming?" Her stomach churned with uncertainty. Six months and this was the first time another living soul besides Holloway and Tanner, then Jax had set foot up here.

Couldn't be good.

"Tanner and one of his deputies are coming up to talk to the man. If he was sent by Armone, hopefully we'll know soon."

"Where are we going?" She told herself not to be nervous. If she had to move again, she would move again. Whatever she had to do to get through this.

Four more days.

"Away from here." He ushered her and Bob toward his SUV. "We're not waiting around to see how this turns out."

Chapter Four

Jax drove faster than he should on the narrow dirt-and-gravel road that would lead to the main highway at the bottom of the mountain. This was not the place to run into trouble. The road was only wide enough for one vehicle. If someone else appeared on the road...

He wasn't going there just yet.

From the corner of his eye, he saw Ali struggling with the panic no doubt clawing at her. She was worried. She had a right to be. *He* was damned worried.

He didn't take a deep breath until they hit the Y in the road. Left went up another mountain road, while the right went to the highway. He gunned the accelerator and barreled to the right. Ali grasped the armrest on her door.

Car lights on the road ahead had him holding his breath again.

The vehicle passed. No brake lights lit up in the rearview mirror. Good. The driver kept going.

"What do we do now? Are we going someplace specific?"

He glanced in her direction. "I don't know. I'm not familiar with this area. You?"

She shook her head. "No. I've been here six months, but I've only left that mountain a couple of times."

They drove on through the darkness, the silence thickening.

Tanner would call and they would make a plan. Until then, Jax would drive.

"Could I go to the hospital and see Marshal Holloway?"

Her question gave him pause. Sometimes witnesses grew very attached to the people assigned with the responsibility of their protection. He'd heard stories of bizarre obsessions, but he didn't believe this was one of those times. She'd asked about his condition after she learned of the accident, but she hadn't appeared unduly concerned. Maybe a stop at the hospital would get her mind off whatever was going down back at the cabin.

"I don't see why not." He reached beyond the console into the back seat and grabbed the ball cap he'd tossed back there and passed it to her. "You might want to tuck your hair up."

"Okay."

As her fingers threaded into all that blond hair, a jolt of tension roared through him. His mind instantly conjured dozens of images of him running his fingers through the silky length. Feeling the whisper of it against his skin.

He blinked away the images and focused on regaining his bearings. He'd driven from the hospital to the sheriff's office and then here. But that had been in the daytime. There weren't that many identifying road signs.

A few more miles had him reasonably certain he was lost. Then he spotted the sign he needed. Left to Winchester. It wasn't long after that left when he began to see familiar landmarks. The drive to the hospital only took a few more minutes from the city limits.

Jax decided to park at the ER entrance and go in from there. Ali gave Bob a rub behind the ears. "We'll be back soon, boy."

Jax's thinking was that anyone watching for Ali would more likely be waiting in the main lobby. He wound through the corridors until he found a staff elevator. Ali glanced around nervously as they waited for the doors to open. Once they were inside and moving upward, she seemed to relax.

When the elevator stopped he said, "Almost there."

He didn't know why he felt compelled to make her feel more comfortable. He'd told himself he wouldn't feel anything like that toward her, but he did all the same. The doors opened, and a scrub-clad woman stared at them as they exited. Jax gave her a nod and kept walking. Ali stayed close behind him.

At the room where he'd visited Holloway earlier that day, he hesitated and knocked.

The door opened, and a man Jax didn't recognize looked directly at him and asked, "Can I help you?"

Jax glanced at the bed about the same time Holloway said, "It's Stevens. Let him in."

They walked into the room, and the stranger closed the door behind them. Holloway frowned. "What's going on, Stevens?" He gave Ali a tip of his head. "Ma'am, you okay?"

She nodded. "I wanted to see if you were okay and to speak to you. Privately."

"I should probably go," the stranger said. He thrust his hand toward Jax. "I'm Chief of Police Billy Brannigan."

Jax shook his hand. "Jaxson Stevens."

"The marshal who's filling in for me," Holloway explained to the chief. "Keeping a low profile," he added as he shifted his attention to Jax.

"We had a guy claiming to be from the utility company show up. Tanner is checking him out. I didn't want to hang around in case more trouble was headed our way."

"Maybe I ought to check with Colt and see if he needs any help," Brannigan offered.

"Thanks, Brannigan. I would appreciate it."

"In that case, I'm gone."

When the door closed behind Brannigan, Holloway looked from Jax to Ali. "Is something wrong besides your unexpected visitor?"

"I'd like to speak to you privately," she repeated.

Jax got it now. "I'll be outside."

If the woman didn't want him on the case, he wasn't going to argue with her. She could do as she pleased.

He left the room, pulling the door closed behind him. Rather than pace the corridor, which was his first thought, he leaned against the wall and waited.

Frustration twisted inside him. He supposed he should have handled the situation better. He'd thought they had reached an agreement of sorts. He would do his job and stay out of her personal space. Four days. It was barely more than half a week. He could get through four days. Why couldn't she?

Damn it all to hell. He shouldn't have allowed the past to color his attitude. This was an important case. She needed the best protecting her.

Maybe she didn't think he was up to the job.

He resisted the impulse to storm into the room and tell her she was wrong. There wasn't anyone better.

Damn it.

"HAVE A SEAT, ALI," Marshal Holloway said, worry lining his bruised face.

Ali suddenly regretted having come here this way. It was selfish of her to impose upon this injured man. She sighed. Closed her eyes for a moment. "I'm sorry."

"First off, you don't need to be sorry."

She opened her eyes. "Are you sure you're okay?

I really should have thought this through better. This is not a good time for you and—"

"Second," he interrupted, "every single thing related to this case is about you. Whatever you need, all you have to do is tell me. Marshal Stevens or I will make it happen. You can count on that."

"Marshal Stevens is the problem." Her throat ached from having held the words back so long. But they were out there now. Marshal Holloway looked even more puzzled now.

"Is there a problem with Stevens? He mentioned that the two of you knew each other, but he assured me there wouldn't be a problem."

Now she was the one confused. "He knew I was the witness in this case before he came to Winchester?"

"No, ma'am, we've kept your identity and location as deeply covered as possible. He learned who you are when he arrived and I showed him your file."

So he'd seen her file. A cold hard knot formed in her chest. "Everything?" She moistened her lips and tried to swallow to do the same to her suddenly dry throat. "He knows everything?"

His blue eyes lit with understanding. "No. No. None of that is in the file I showed him. Ali, those parts of what happened aren't necessary for Marshal Stevens to carry out his duty. Information about you and this case is on a need-to-know basis."

Thank God.

She nodded. Grateful for that small measure of relief. "Still, I would prefer someone else. I don't want to cause any trouble for Marshal Stevens, but I'm not comfortable with him."

Holloway released a big breath. "I can make the call and try to get someone here, but be aware that every exchange of information creates a possible opportunity for that information to end up in the wrong hands. It's a shame that we can't fully trust all the players in a case, but they're only human. Every human has his or her breaking point. Some have a price. It doesn't usually start out that way, but life happens. People change."

He was right. She understood this. She wasn't completely naive to these sorts of things. Harrison and his father had had only a few they trusted with everything. The rest were only allowed a tiny piece of knowledge—only what was required to carry out their mission.

But she had to be firm. This was what she wanted. "I apologize for making this difficult for you, Marshal Holloway—especially under the circumstances—but I'm willing to take the risk. I would like you to send Marshal Stevens back to Nashville."

He studied her a moment. "If you'll tell me the real reason you want him to go, I promise I'll make it happen if that is truly what you want."

The real reason. She glanced back at the door. She had promised herself that she would never allow lies into her life again. If that rule didn't start with her, what was the point?

"We both know there is a strong chance Armone's

people will find me no matter what we do or how careful we are." When he would have interrupted, she held up a hand to stop him. "It may be as I walk up the steps at the courthouse or as I enter the courtroom." She shrugged. "In the car on the way to the airport. At the airport. There are just a million opportunities for it to happen."

The weariness and probably pain he struggled with filled his expression, but Holloway nodded his understanding. "You're right. It's possible one of those scenarios could happen. Are you having second thoughts?"

Startled by his question, she pressed her hand to her chest. "No. Not at all. Whatever happens, I'm going to testify as long as I'm still breathing. It's not me I'm worried about. It's him."

Realization dawned on his face. "You're concerned that if they come after you, anyone in the way will be hurt or worse."

"Yes. I don't want to cause *him* harm." How did she explain this without sounding like a fool? "I know his family. His mother is a wonderful woman. He has a sister with three kids. I don't want to risk being the cause of his family losing him."

Holloway seemed to consider her explanation for a moment. "Ali, that's incredibly noble of you." He spoke as if he were choosing his words carefully. "But you must be aware that Marshal Stevens risks his life every day on the job. If he leaves this assignment, he'll only go to another that could be even more dangerous."

She couldn't deny the former, but she had her doubts about the latter. Armone, the bastard, was completely ruthless, and he had endless resources. There had to be something she could say that would change his mind. What he'd said to her at the onset bobbed into her frantic thoughts.

"You said whatever I wanted," she reminded him. "All I had to do was ask."

He gave a nod. "You've got me there." He stared at her for a long moment. "Jaxson Stevens is one of the very best. We're very lucky he was available. Anytime there's a touchy situation, he's the one they go to. They would likely have put him on this case instead of me, except he wasn't available then."

He was going to say no. Her hopes fell.

"All that said," he went on, "if you're set on having someone else, I'll make it happen. But I think it would be a mistake. Has he done or said anything to you that has you feeling upset or uncomfortable?"

"No, not really." Truth, she reminded herself. "I was deeply in love with him once." She shrugged. Felt like a fool.

Holloway held up his hand to prevent her from saying more.

"I need to say this," she warned. "The truth is maybe I still am even after all this time. All I know is that I can't allow him to risk his life for me."

"You don't get to make that decision."

Her heart dropped to the floor at the sound of his voice.

Holloway sighed. "I tried to stop you when the door opened."

He had, and she wouldn't listen. Her back was to the door, and she'd had no idea. Oh God, he'd heard her declaration. She told herself it wasn't entirely true…only partly so.

Jax joined her at the marshal's bedside. Ali couldn't look at him. Not after what she'd said. How she wished the floor would crack open and swallow her up. Good grief, could she have stuck her foot any deeper into her throat?

"Ten years," Jax said, his voice oddly neutral. "It's been ten years. We've both moved on. Whatever you think you feel is more likely resentment because I left."

Heat scalded her cheeks even hotter. Lovely. Now Holloway knew the rest of the sad story of their shared history. She and Jax had had an intense relationship ten years ago, until he got an offer he couldn't refuse and then he was gone.

She was a fool. Then and now.

Ali turned to him. "Or maybe you're just feeling guilty for walking away and now you have something to prove."

He moved his head slowly from side to side. "Trust me, I have nothing to prove. You're a witness in a high-profile, very important case. I'm here to make sure you stay alive until you've testified. Nothing more."

Anger fired inside her. She shifted her attention back to Holloway. "Fine. Let him stay. If he gets himself killed, it won't be on me."

Holloway struggled to sit up straighter. Ali winced at the pain on his face.

"I don't like this one damned bit," he said then grimaced, "but we are too close to risk a screwup." He stared at Jax. "Can you handle this?"

"What the hell, Holloway? You know better than to ask."

"Tell me you won't get distracted."

He shook his head. "I will not get distracted. Like I told you, whatever we had was over a long damned time ago."

His words were like a slap to her face. Ali pinched her lips together. Anything else she said at this point would only make her look more foolish.

Holloway slumped against his pillow. "If I could get out of this bed, we would not be having this discussion."

"I've got this, Branch," Jax said, using the marshal's first name.

Apparently the two knew each other better than she had realized.

Jax reached into his jacket pocket and pulled out his cell. "It's Tanner."

He answered the call, explained their situation and set the phone to speaker. "Go ahead, Tanner."

"The man posing as a utilities worker is Rafe Sanford."

Holloway looked from Jax to Ali and back. "Sanford is a local thug. In and out of trouble all the time."

"Always has been," Tanner reiterated. "Mostly petty crimes, but there have been rumors of bigger jobs but no evidence to ever tie him to any of it. I've got him in lockup now. He says a man sought him out and hired him to see if a certain blonde lady was holed up anywhere around town. He suggested Rafe keep an eye on Marshal Holloway and me, as well as Chief Brannigan as a way of finding what he was looking for."

Ali's mortification from what Jax had overheard vanished as her fears were realized. Armone had found her again.

"He says he was caught before he could report back to the guy. He has a cell number to call. He says the guy was wearing a suit like he was some big hotshot. Waited for him at the pool hall. Looked about as out of place as a bald guy at a barbershop."

"Have you confirmed his story?" Jax asked.

"I did. Kenneth Prince, owner of the pool hall, described the same guy hanging out twice this week."

"Is Sanford supposed to meet with him again?"

"Only if he finds her location. He gets one thousand dollars in cash."

Ali felt sick to her stomach. That was the Armone way.

Holloway was trying to sit up again. Jax shook his head and ushered him back down.

"You think we can set up a sting operation?" Holloway asked.

"We?" Jax laughed. "You're not leaving this hospital. I'm taking this witness—" he glanced at Ali "—someplace safe."

"I've already notified the FBI," Tanner said. "They want this guy."

"Damn." Holloway blew out a breath. "The more activity in this area, the more attention we draw."

"Deputy James Carter is headed to your location now. Stevens, he'll take you to a place to stay tonight."

"We need security at Holloway's home and on his room here at the hospital," Jax said.

Ali hated this. She didn't want anyone else hurt because of that bastard.

Holloway protested. "I don't need—"

"Don't argue," Jax ordered.

"Making that happen now," Tanner said. "We can't be sure what this man knows. If Sanford doesn't come through for him, he may move onto bigger fish."

Holloway muttered a curse.

While Tanner and Jax continued to talk, Holloway looked at Ali. "You okay?"

She managed a nod. "You guys have the tough job. All I have to do is stay alive."

Falls Mills Bed & Breakfast

SHERIFF TANNER WAS friends with the owner of the historic bed-and-breakfast. Since there were no guests tonight, he had turned the place over to Tanner.

The bed-and-breakfast was a small two-story

cabin built in the late 1800s, according to the brochure on the table by the door. The location was sort of off-the-grid. Not as much as the cabin where she'd stayed for the past six months, but definitely on a road less traveled.

She glanced at the clock—almost nine. Not so late, but she was exhausted. The owner had closed and locked the gate to the main property. Of course that wouldn't stop a man like Armone.

"Here we go."

Jax was on one knee in front of the fireplace; Bob watched him intently, his tail wagging. Jax had started a fire. He had a bit of trouble in the beginning. Ali had thought about telling him that she could do it, but she'd decided to avoid conversation as much as possible. She did not want him to ask her about what she'd said to Holloway. She'd come up with an excuse to explain it away, but she'd rather not talk about it.

Ever.

He stood. "You hungry? Tanner said the place was stocked. We can have a look, see what's available."

"I think I'll just go to bed." She needed some time alone to regroup and pull herself together.

She could not linger here any longer and have him stare at her the way he was right this second.

"We eat and then we sack out."

"Okay." She started toward the kitchen, moving past him as quickly as possible. Bob trailed behind her.

Jax followed. She didn't have to look back—she

could feel his nearness. How could she be so keenly aware of him after all these years?

To distract herself from him and to get this whole eating thing over, she perused the cabinets and the fridge in the small kitchen. Nothing she saw made her the slightest bit hungry. But he was right. She had to eat or she wouldn't be able to function at her best. She grabbed a can of soup and crackers along with a bottle of water. While he prowled, she heated her soup in the microwave. There was no dog food, so she opened a can of little sausages for Bob. Then she went to sit on the floor by the fire.

She couldn't get warm.

She needed a shower. A toothbrush and clothes.

It felt as if this nightmare was never going to be over. She forced herself to eat the soup and munch on a cracker. It would be nice to say she couldn't wait to go home, but she had no home. She had nothing. Not even a vehicle. The one at the cabin didn't belong to her.

Nothing belonged to her. Not even the few items of clothing in the bureau in that cabin she would never see again.

Tears burned her eyes, but she refused to cry. Crying was pointless. Besides, she was utterly exhausted. She lacked the energy to cry.

Every family photo she possessed was at the house she had shared with Harrison. The necklace her father had given her for her sixteenth birthday, the watch her mother had worn every day of her life and dozens of other mementos.

Armone had probably had them destroyed.

He would love hurting her that way. Bastard.

"About the thing at the hospital."

She dropped the spoon into her empty bowl. Somehow, she had finished the soup. "What thing?"

"What you were saying to Holloway."

He was staring at her. Waiting for her to look at him. She refused. Kept her gaze locked on the bottle of water in her hand. "I said what I thought I had to say to get him to take you off the case."

It was a good excuse and kept her from looking totally pathetic.

"I see." He scooped up another spoonful of cereal.

"Good night." She got to her feet and started toward the kitchen with her bowl.

"For the record," he said.

She stopped but didn't look back.

"It doesn't matter. This is what I do. Nothing more."

She took another step and then another until she reached the kitchen. Careful not to drop the bowl, she placed it in the sink, her hand shaking. The crackers went back into the cabinet. He came into the kitchen and placed his bowl in the sink next to hers. She braced herself for walking past him once more.

"Good night," he said as she passed.

She kept walking, Bob on her heels.

Chapter Five

Three days until trial

Monday, February 3

A sound woke her.

The room was pitch-dark. Ali lay still and listened. The distant sound of the falls, the occasional splat of something wet against the metal roof. More snow?

She had no idea what time it was.

Throwing the handmade quilt aside, she sat up. Her bare feet settled on the cold wood floor. Her eyes slowly adjusted to the darkness. Across the room the other bed was empty. The white linens beneath the other handmade quilt confirmed her conclusion.

Where was Jax?

Maybe he'd awakened early and gone down for coffee. Ali drew in a deep breath. Since the loft was open on one side to the first level, the scent of brewed coffee would surely have wafted up to her.

No hint of coffee lingered in the air. Just the cold

air flavored with the slightest scent of lavender. There were bunches of the dried herb neatly placed throughout the room. Pushing up to her feet, she righted her clothes. The sweatshirt had twisted around her waist, and the jeans had crawled up above her ankles. Somewhere around the bed were her socks and shoes. She should find them before going downstairs. She moved slowly around the bed, swiping one soundless foot across the wood until she bumped the pile of abandoned footwear.

Where was Bob?

Settling on the floor, she gathered the socks first and tugged them on. Then the shoes that were her favorites. This was the only footwear she'd brought with her when she walked away from that gym. When this was over, she would certainly need to refresh her wardrobe.

Assuming she needed something more than a burial dress.

She shivered. The cold, she told herself. She wasn't afraid. Not really. Especially now. She was far more afraid of Jax being hurt than she was of her own mortality. She had bought in to this tragic nightmare. He had not. He was only attempting to do his job. She cringed at the memory of him hearing what she'd said to Marshal Holloway. It wasn't true, of course. The assurance rang hollowly in her head. Yes, she had feelings for him. He had been her first love. But she wasn't still *in* love with him.

Not possible.

She got up and moved quietly to the stairs. They were narrow, not made for more than one person at a time. Downstairs was just as dark as upstairs. She opened her mouth to call his name, but some deeply entrenched instinct stopped her.

It was too quiet.

If he was up, why wasn't a light on? Why didn't she smell coffee?

Another step downward and then another. Maybe he'd gone outside to look around. Check the perimeter or whatever bodyguards did.

She took the final step down to the lower level and turned toward the kitchen area. Moonlight filtered in through the window. No Jax.

A firm hand closed over her mouth. Her scream lodged in her throat.

A strong arm locked around her and flattened her against a hard body. "Quiet," he whispered.

Jax.

Thank God.

Holding her tight against him, he shuffled soundlessly away from the stairs and the meager light trickling into the kitchen.

When they were in the darkest corner of the room, his mouth brushed her ear again. She shivered, and it had nothing to do with the cold.

"There's someone outside."

Her pulse accelerated. She pinched her lips together to prevent any sound from escaping. Holloway had been right. The closer the trial date got, the more desperate Armone would become. All these months had been so quiet, so uneventful. She closed her eyes and focused on steadying her breathing.

Where was Bob? She opened her mouth to ask, but the dog's warm body brushed against her leg, alleviating the need. Her fingers trailed the length of his back.

Jax guided her to the area beneath the narrow stairs. Bob scooted in next to her. Jax touched her lips with one finger in the universal sign for quiet.

As he moved away, she lost sight of him in the darkness. The other windows in the cabin, including the one in the door, were covered with curtains. Jax had carefully closed them all when they first arrived. Only the kitchen window was uncovered. If trouble was here, they needed backup. He shouldn't do this alone.

She reached into the hip pocket of her jeans, thankful her phone was still tucked there. Squatting deeper beneath the stairs, she turned it on and waited for the home screen to appear. Her fingers shaking, she quickly typed a text message to Holloway.

SOS

The promising dots that he was responding appeared, and she held her breath.

Relief swam through her veins. A thumbs-up meant he had received the message and would send help. Since there were two thumbs-up images, she assumed Jax had already called for assistance.

Everything would be okay. *If* they arrived in time. As far as she could tell driving in the dark last night, they were sort of in the middle of nowhere.

A scratching sound whispered through the darkness.

The air trapped in her lungs.

The urge to rush out there and help in some way hurtled through her.

Be still!

This entire case depended on her survival to testify. If something happened to her, the old bastard would get away with everything the same way he had for decades.

She could not allow that to happen.

Glass shattered at the front of the cabin. Next to her, Bob's body tensed. The door opened.

Ali twisted just enough to see beyond the stair treads. The staircase was open with no risers or anything that would block her view.

With the door open, moonlight arrowed across the floor. The instinct to draw away nudged her, but she didn't dare move. A shadow blocked the light.

Her heart bolted against her sternum. Bob pressed closer against her, his fur standing up. She gave him the hand signal to stay. He was trained not to move or to make a sound when given that signal.

The slightest brush of a shoe sole against the hardwood. Then another and another. He—whoever he was—moved about in the darkness. Ali held her breath. Tried to make herself as small as possible.

The sigh of his weight settling onto the first tread sent fear roaring through her.

Another brush of rubber against wood as he braced a shoe on the next step.

A grunt echoed in the darkness.

The tread squeaked with movement.

For a moment there were only grunting sounds and fabric rustling. She tried to make out what was happening, but she could only see movement in the darkness. It was impossible to discern what she was looking at other than she understood the two men were struggling.

"Do not move."

Jax.

His order was directed at the other man. Bob issued a low growl.

Again, the urge to get out there and help somehow prodded at her.

Blue lights suddenly throbbed in the darkness.

Backup had arrived.

"On your feet," Jax instructed.

With the headlights of the official vehicles shining on the cabin, she could see the man scramble to his feet.

"Hands behind your head."

He obeyed Jax's command.

Tanner and two uniformed deputies filed in through the door. Chief Brannigan followed. Someone flipped on the overhead light. Ali squinted until her eyes adjusted to the brightness.

"Everything okay?" Tanner asked.

Jax nodded. "Just caught this scumbag trying to slip in and mess up my vacation."

The last was an effort to throw the man off. No one wanted him reporting back to whoever hired him that he had indeed found the witness.

Tanner cuffed the man's hands behind his back.

"I have a few questions for him before you take him away," Jax said.

"Let's step outside and have a chat," Tanner suggested.

Flashlights bobbed in the night. Ali supposed there were other deputies out there searching the area. There was always the possibility that this guy hadn't come alone.

Before walking out, Jax said something to Brannigan for his ears only.

When the door closed, Brannigan came around to the back of the staircase and couched down. "You all right, ma'am?"

Bob's tail thumped on the wood floor as if he recognized one of the good guys.

"Yes." The word was rusty. She managed her first deep breath since waking up.

"I think it's safe for you to come out now." He offered his hand.

Ali put her hand in his and scrambled from her hiding place, Bob right behind her.

"Thank you."

"Anytime."

Brannigan was like Tanner and Holloway. He wore the cowboy boots and the hat. He had the same polite manners, as well. All this time she'd believed cowboys were overrated. Maybe not. Her mind was whirling with silly thoughts and ideas. She was too tired and too stressed and coming down off an adrenaline rush fueled by fear. On cue, her knees attempted to buckle.

"Steady there." Brannigan took her by the arm and ushered her to the nearest chair.

She sat, managed another thanks. When she'd composed herself a bit, she asked, "Do we know if he's one of Armone's men?"

"I figure we'll know that any minute now."

He was probably right.

The phone still clutched in her hand vibrated.

She looked at the screen.

?

Holloway wanted to know if she was okay. She sent him a thumbs-up, and he shot back a smiley face.

She suddenly felt tremendously lucky to have been stashed in Winchester. Everyone had been so nice to her. It wasn't at all like her first location, where she'd felt like a prisoner, an outsider…a criminal.

Before she could stop the reaction, tears spilled

down her cheeks. She felt like a complete idiot. Bob set his head on her knees and stared at her with sad eyes.

Brannigan crouched down beside her chair. "Hey, now. We've got the situation under control. No need for tears."

He stood and crossed the room, came back with a box of tissues.

She pulled out a couple and swabbed at her cheeks. "Sorry. I guess I was due for a little breakdown."

"I'm certain of it," he assured her. "We all need a way to blow off steam from time to time. There's no rule that says you can't do it this way."

She sucked in a big breath and attempted to compose herself.

"You need a place to stay until we figure out what happens next," he said. "I thought you and the marshal could stay in town at the funeral home."

"Funeral home?" A frown pulled at her weary face.

"Several generations of DuPonts grew up there," he said with a smile. "I live there with Rowan DuPont. But there's plenty of room in the living quarters above the funeral home. You'll be safe there."

She'd expected to possibly end up in a funeral home before this was over. She just hadn't expected to be alive.

Jax made sure Ali and Bob were tucked in for the night before going into the living room. Chief Brannigan waited for him. He'd introduced Rowan DuPont, the owner of the funeral home, to them when they first arrived an hour ago. She had gone to bed soon after, up on the third floor. Brannigan had explained that Rowan's family had built the funeral home more than a century and a half ago. DuPonts had lived on the second and third floors since. Rowan was the only one left now.

Jax had heard about her. Before her father's death, Rowan had worked with Nashville Metro. A serial killer had become infatuated with her and murdered her father. In fact, the bastard was still out there, haunting her from afar.

Sometimes it felt like the bad guys won too often. Kept guys like him fighting an uphill battle.

"Tanner brought me up to speed on the case," Brannigan said. "He and Holloway will have a new safe house for the two of you by daylight."

Jax nodded. "Good. I'll need to inspect my vehicle more closely in the light of day first. The guy pretending to be from the utility company, Teddy Scott, stuck a tracker on my SUV. If I hadn't been in such a hurry to get out of there I would have thought of that and checked first."

He wasn't sure he could forgive himself for that mistake. Ali could have been killed. The bastard he'd taken down wouldn't talk other than to demand a call to his lawyer. A quick cell phone pic sent to a deputy at the jail, and Scott had confirmed the man was the same one who had hired him to look for Ali.

Armone hadn't sent him. He was a damned investigative reporter from Atlanta. Jax had known something was off when the man broke the glass in the door. What kind of hired killer announced his presence by busting his way inside?

There was always the chance he had a team with him, in which case it wouldn't have mattered, but one man alone would have wanted to keep his presence unknown for as long as possible.

Outrage rushed through him again just thinking about the kind of person who would put a photo op before a person's life—including his own.

"I have people who can help with going over your vehicle," Brannigan assured him.

"I appreciate your support, Chief." Jax couldn't remember the last time he'd felt so tired. Lots of cases were tough, but this one was taking it out of him fast.

Doesn't have anything to do with the identity of the witness.

The lie echoed in his brain.

Brannigan shook his head. "The dead husband was one sick puppy."

Jax knew a great deal about the man professionally, but he knew very little about his personal life. One of the reasons the bastards had escaped justice so long was because of their ability to keep their personal lives as tight as a vault.

"Most of them are." He'd never met a criminal at Armone's level who was anything but pure evil.

"Frankly, I don't see how she survived. It took real courage not to just take the easy way out and end the pain."

What the hell was he talking about? "I don't know what you mean."

Ali had married Harrison Armone of her own volition. Had stayed married to him for five years.

"You didn't read the file?"

"I read the file Holloway showed me at the hospital, but there wasn't any information about the relationship between her and him other than the fact that she was his widow."

Surprise flashed across Brannigan's face, but he quickly schooled his expression. "I see."

Jax went inordinately still. "You read a different file."

It wasn't a question. What he had been shown was the bare minimum. After all, he was a US marshal, the same as Holloway. He knew who and what the Armone family was. He hadn't needed all the dirty details.

"I was made aware of additional information." Brannigan stood. "I think I'll try to get a couple more hours of shut-eye. You should do the same."

Jax stood. "I'd like to know what you saw that I didn't."

Brannigan held his gaze for a moment. "You should talk to Holloway about that, or maybe the lady in question. Good night, Stevens."

He headed for the stairs that would take him to the third floor.

Jax walked down the hall to the room where Ali slept. Rowan had explained that it had been her parents' room. The night-light in the hall cast a dim glow into the room and across the bed. Ali slept soundly.

What had she been through that she didn't want him to know? Not just her. Obviously, Holloway had made the decision that passing along those personal details wasn't necessary for Jax to do his job. And it wasn't.

But he wanted to know.

His gut tied up in knots when he considered the possibilities. There were some sick individuals in this world.

He couldn't help wondering if he'd stayed in Georgia with her if he could have...

He pushed away the thought. He couldn't undo the past. He wasn't even sure he would want to if he could.

Before he started kicking himself for that long-ago decision, he needed to know the truth. He had regretted his decision on some level, sure. He'd been crazy about her ten years ago. He'd wanted to spend forever with her. Whatever forever meant to a twenty-two-year-old guy with a burning desire to save the world.

She had only wanted to get through college. She'd had to delay starting for more than a year after high school to help her father take care of her mother. After her mother passed, she'd resumed her plan. That was how they'd met. She was in college and he'd been at Glynco, and they'd ended up at the same pizza place.

She was the prettiest girl he'd ever seen and so

shy. The shyness had really intrigued him. He'd had to dig for every nugget of information. She was the only woman he'd ever taken home to meet his family.

His mother and sister had adored Ali. His father, too. He'd told Jax that she was the one. At twenty-two, who listens to their old man?

The whole family had been upset with him when he moved to Seattle alone. On some level he had known it was a mistake, as well. But he hadn't taken steps to make it right until it was too late and she'd married a monster. He hadn't allowed her to creep into his thoughts again…until yesterday.

No point beating a dead horse. It was done. It was over. She was the one who'd married someone else.

He checked the door locks and the security system key pad then slipped quietly into the room where she slept. Bob was stretched out on the floor next to the bed. He lifted his head, eyed Jax for a moment, then relaxed on the floor once more. Jax went into the en suite bath and closed the door before turning on the light.

Rowan had supplied fresh towels and toiletries. He placed his weapon and cell phone on the floor next to the shower, turned on the water and shed his clothes and shoes. He stepped under the hot spray and just stood there for a while, allowing the water to slide over his body.

Every muscle tightened when he thought of the way Ali's body had felt against his when he'd pulled her to him to whisper in her ear. Even under the circumstances, he had felt that old familiar need to keep holding her, to turn her around and to kiss her the way he used to.

He didn't want to feel that way. Not after she'd lived with a man like Armone.

Scrubbing the soap over his body, he tried his level best to banish thoughts of her, but she wasn't going anywhere.

He thought of the comment Brannigan had made. Had he been wrong all these years?

No. He let the hot water wash away the soap then he reached for the shampoo. She'd married the bastard because she wanted to. No one forced her. He'd seen them together.

The idea that he had watched her for days five years ago after he had discovered she was married was another of those memories he would like to evict from his head. No matter that he had been the one to walk away, he had somehow always expected to end up with Ali. When she finished school, if he still felt as strongly about her, he would hunt her down and sweep her off her feet. Dazzle her and change her mind about moving to the northwest. He'd wanted that time and distance to give her a chance to decide what she really wanted. He had been certain his shy, small-town love wasn't going anywhere. She would be waiting for him. Only he'd been wrong.

He had been an arrogant fool.

She had found someone new.

He had made the mistake of his life.

She was just as pretty as he remembered, but she was with *him*.

He'd told himself that she couldn't possibly understand what kind of man Armone was, but his pride had overrode any doubt or sympathy,

He turned off the water and climbed out of the shower. That was the part that didn't add up. Why would she even go out with a man like Armone? Didn't she recognize evil when she saw it?

She couldn't possibly have married him without at least some idea of who he was.

This was the part he couldn't overlook. That really got to him. That he couldn't forgive.

She hadn't looked back, either. Hadn't tried to call him. Hadn't called his mom or his sister. She had just gone on with her life and married someone else. That part was on him. No denying it.

He toweled off and pulled his clothes back on. Whatever Brannigan knew that he didn't wouldn't make any difference.

Maybe that made him heartless, but if you didn't want to be bitten, you didn't climb into a den of snakes.

Chapter Six

A dusting of snow had fallen during the wee hours before daylight.

Ali stared out the window over the yard behind the funeral home. Funny, it looked like any other backyard. Freud, Rowan's German shepherd, pranced around the yard as if he wanted to make as many footprints in the snow as possible.

But this was no typical residence. Downstairs people were prepared for their final journey in this life. Funerals and wakes were carried out. She shivered. How fitting that she would be in this place. Her life the past five years had been nothing more than a facade for a dead marriage to a killer.

With a shudder, she pushed the thought away. She'd stirred at some point just before daylight. Jax had been sleeping in a chair on the other side of the bedroom. A lamp on the table next to the chair had cast a soft glow over his face.

Taking care not to make a sound, she had sat up in bed and watched him for a long while. The few lines around his eyes had relaxed in sleep. A day's beard growth shadowed his jaw. She didn't want to smile, but her lips formed the expression, anyway. He had hardly changed. Still good-looking. A little leaner in places, more heavily muscled in others. The boy right out of college and psyched about attending marshal training had been full of energy and excitement. This Jax was all man. All grown-up and slightly jaded after a decade in his chosen career.

He was quieter…more still. She suspected all that energy and excitement had calmed a bit and that the newer, deeper emotions were kept close, behind the tin star he carried. But in sleep, he looked so much like the very young man she had fallen so hard for. She had been so naive, which was kind of sad, since she hadn't started college until she was twenty. Certainly she hadn't been the starry-eyed eighteen-year-old fresh out of high school. Ali had spent two years taking care of her mother before she passed away. She'd barely gotten three years of college under her belt when her father had fallen ill. Another year at home with him, and then she'd found herself completely alone. Those final two semesters of college had been so lonely. Moving to the big city had seemed like the perfect change.

Instead, it had been the biggest mistake of her life.

Somehow she'd drifted off to sleep again, and now she dreaded leaving this quiet room. She'd heard people stirring. Heard the low rumble of Jax's voice as well as the softer voice of a woman. Rowan Du-

Pont, she imagined. Ali had met her only briefly last night. Like Ali, she had long blond hair. She, too, had that look in her eyes—the one that said she had experienced deep pain.

Ali righted her sweatshirt and smoothed a hand over her jeans-clad hips. Bob waited by the door watching her. He was probably starving. Rowan had a dog, too. Thankfully Freud hadn't seemed to mind the company—not even Bob. The two dogs had eyed each other speculatively but neither bothered to growl.

Ali needed fresh clothes. Hopefully, Sheriff Tanner could bring her clothes from the cabin. She slipped on her shoes and ran a brush through her hair again. Then she headed out to learn what would happen next.

The living room was empty. Listening for the voices, she followed the sound into the kitchen. Both Jax and Rowan turned her way as she entered the room.

"Good morning." Rowan smiled. "The coffee is strong and hot, and Billy made breakfast before he had to head to the office."

A chief of police who cooked. Judging by Rowan's smile, she was very happy that he did. "Thank you."

Jax poured a mug full of the steaming brew and passed it to her. She thanked him.

"There's cream and sugar," Rowan said, "if you don't like it black."

"Black is fine." Ali noticed that Jax remembered.

She kept her gaze away from his for fear he would recognize that she had noticed.

Rowan crossed the room and picked up a plastic bowl filled with kibbles and placed it on the floor. "Bob," she said to the dog, "this is for you."

Bob trotted over to the bowl and dug in.

"Thank you," Ali said to her, immensely grateful for the extra mile.

Rowan smiled. "Well, I have a client coming at nine. I should probably start preparations."

"Thank you so much for your hospitality," Ali offered. She was immensely grateful to all the people who had gone to such lengths to help her do this.

"Good luck, Ali," Rowan said. "You're doing the right thing."

Ali nodded and watched her go. She wondered at the things the woman had been forced to do in her life. There was a sadness about her, but it didn't overwhelm her. Ali hoped the past few years would not define her for the rest of her life.

She stared at the lovely breakfast spread across the counter. Eggs, biscuits, bacon. Her stomach knotted at the thought of eating.

"You have to eat."

She turned to the man, who could clearly still read her like an open book. "I'm really not hungry."

"You're going to need all the strength and courage you can muster. To do that, you need to eat."

"What about you?"

"I've already eaten."

She gathered a plate and fork and went through the motions, forcing herself to consume a few bites of egg and a biscuit. Once she started, her appetite roused and kept the ordeal from being entirely awful.

The coffee gave her a shot of energy, chasing away the lingering shadows from last night's drama.

"How long will we be staying here?" It wasn't the idea of the funeral home below that bothered her. The trouble was that her presence put Rowan and anyone else here in danger. Ali didn't want anyone to suffer because of her.

"Tanner and Holloway should have a new safe house for us in a few hours. The last time we spoke, he was going to check out a location."

She downed the last gulp of her coffee. "What about my clothes from the cabin? Is there any chance he can bring those?"

"One of his deputies brought your things to the sheriff's office. They'll be at the new location when we arrive."

"Great." She needed a shower. She needed clean clothes and some time away from the rest of the world.

This time three days from now, she would be sitting in a courtroom preparing to testify against old man Armone. It seemed strange that the idea of testifying didn't scare her. She looked forward to the opportunity. Worry about who would get hurt ensuring she had that opportunity gnawed at her relentlessly. She thought of Marshal Holloway and his wife and daughter. Sheriff Tanner and his family. She thought of Chief Brannigan and Rowan. And she thought of Jax.

So many people who could be hurt.

Rather than dwell on the worrisome thoughts, she busied herself cleaning up. She tucked the dirty dishes into the dishwasher. Someone had already cleaned the stove and washed the cooking utensils. There was really nothing else she could do in here. Rather than try making amiable conversation with Jax, she went back to the bedroom and made up the bed.

When she was finished, she lingered. The desk in the room was covered with dozens of notebooks. She walked closer and decided the notebooks were journals. This had been Rowan's parents' room. They were both gone now. She wondered if the journals were her mother's.

She touched an open page, traced the handwriting. Her own mother hadn't kept a journal. But she had meticulously documented each photo in the family photo albums. Time and place and a note about whatever was happening. Her father had been far more pragmatic. He was eternally focused on work and what needed to be done next. A farmer's life was challenging. Hard work, lots of worry and rarely a decent payoff for the two.

Certain she had sequestered herself in this room for as long as possible without risking Jax showing up to check on her, she walked back into the living room. He was in the kitchen, his low voice and the cell phone tucked against his ear telling her he'd heard from someone. Perhaps there was news about what happened next.

Then again, it could be a personal call. He'd said he'd never married and had never been engaged—which was not entirely true—but that didn't mean he was without a girlfriend. He could have someone up in Nashville waiting for him to come home. The idea hadn't even entered her mind. She had expected him to be married and have a kid or two. That he was not had thrown her for a bit of a loop. Maybe he enjoyed the bachelor lifestyle too much.

He was only thirty-two. He could certainly enjoy a decade more of the single life before bothering to settle down. Made life far less complicated. As a marshal, he could be gone for days or weeks at a time. Without a wife or children to worry about, he was free as a bird.

He hadn't been pathetically needy and lonesome the way she had been.

Bob most likely needed to go outside and do his business. It was possible Jax had taken him out earlier, but she couldn't be sure. She didn't see any reason why she couldn't take him out.

"Come," she said to the animal as she patted her leg.

Bob trotted over, and the two of them exited the living quarters, heading for the staircase. Since there was a fenced backyard, she wouldn't have to worry about the leash. At the top of the stairs, she looked down at the lobby. The place was certainly grand enough. Behind her a towering stained-glass window depicted angels ascending toward heaven. As she descended the staircase, she surveyed the numerous elegant sitting areas—conversation groupings of furniture. The double entrance doors were equally grand.

It really was a beautiful place.

"Hey, Ali."

She turned to Rowan, who was walking toward her down a corridor. On the wall, arrows pointed to that corridor showing that the lounge and restrooms as well as the office were in that direction.

"Hi. I thought I should take Bob out, if it's okay."

"Of course. Follow me."

Rowan led the way through a set of doors labeled Staff Only. Another corridor seemed to lead to the back of the house. Doors lined the corridor, but none were labeled. Toward the end was an elevator. Next to the back door was another set of double doors and a second staircase, this one rather narrow.

Her guide opened the back door and waited for Bob to trot out across the porch.

She watched him for a moment then smiled at Ali. "He'll be fine outside. Did you need anything else?"

Ali shook her head. "No, thank you. I'll just wait here to let him in."

"All right."

Rowan walked away, and Ali's gaze returned to the backyard.

Bob and Freud were prancing around in the snow.

She would love to go out there and join them, but it wouldn't be safe.

For nine months now, everything had revolved around keeping her safe. She'd lived like a recluse. Barely setting foot outside where anyone might see her. Bob had been her only constant companion.

If she survived this, she wanted to do more with her life. Have a real career. Make a difference.

Have a family.

The idea that Jax's face came immediately to mind when she thought of family warned that she was in more danger than anyone knew.

THE HOUSE WAS rustic like a cabin but with all the amenities of a contemporary home. It sat deep in the woods, high on a hillside. To reach the house, Jax had to drive across a stream and up a steep, curvy road that was just barely wide enough to accommodate his SUV. The narrow road had been carved out of the mountainside. Looking over the edge might have been a little unsettling if not for the dense, soaring trees on both sides. Many were bare for the winter, but many more were evergreens and blocked the view of the dirt track from the paved road below.

Not that Jax was particularly worried about anyone finding them too quickly. The right he'd taken off Highway 64 as they neared Huntland had wound deep into the countryside. The only sign of civilization was the worn-out asphalt that was just shy of two actual lanes and the occasional farmhouse. They drove for miles without seeing a thing except trees and that faded asphalt snaking out ahead of them before a small white house surrounded by barns two or three times its size and sweeping pastures appeared. More trees followed.

This, Jax decided, was the sticks. He made a left just past the curve Tanner had described. If possible, this road was even less populated. Trees, trees and more trees. He spotted the wide stream, ice crusting its outer edge. The temperature hadn't risen high enough to melt off the snow. It clung to the branches of trees and the landscape like a coating of powdered sugar on the chocolate cake his mom made every year at Christmas. The memory had his stomach rumbling. Breakfast had been hours ago.

After a meeting with Holloway and Tanner, they sat in on a conference call with the AUSA from Nashville, Adam Knowles. He and his counterpart in Atlanta had decided that a conference call was necessary to ensure Ali was ready for trial. Tomorrow morning at eleven they were to be in Nashville at the AUSA's office.

Jax didn't like it. He didn't like it one damned bit. Holloway was mad as hell. He'd refused at first, but eventually the AUSA had won him over. Now it was up to Jax to take all sorts of back roads and unexpected routes to get Ali to the man's office. She hadn't objected. She'd basically agreed to whatever he suggested. Even her damned attorney, who was also on the call, hadn't objected.

Who the hell was the guy working for?

Still furious, Jax unloaded the last of their supplies from his SUV. This house and its forty mountainous acres belonged to a close friend of Tanner's. It was unoccupied just now, but the power remained on for insurance purposes. The house remained furnished, since the family used it from time to time when they visited their hometown. Just beyond the house, a large water tank sat on a towering stand and gathered water from the underground streams coming from the mountainside. The house also had a generator and a basement.

All the comforts of home—and fully self-sustainable.

Tanner had provided Jax with additional ammo and an extra handgun. Jax had turned on the lights downstairs and checked the two bedrooms upstairs. There was a bathroom upstairs and down. A big kitchen and nice-size family room. The fireplace was huge. Firewood was stacked on the back porch.

It was almost like a vacation rental, except it wasn't.

Ali stood by the fire he'd started as if she couldn't get warm after walking around the property to get familiar with the territory.

"You hungry?" She hadn't eaten much at breakfast.

"I'm good with a peanut butter sandwich." She turned and walked toward the kitchen.

Bob looked at him before following her.

He did the same. "Peanut butter it is, then."

Food wasn't usually such a dominating subject on his mind, but it was a topic he could broach with her without worrying where it might lead.

After she had prepared her sandwich, he did the same. While he placed two slices of bread on a napkin, she went to a fridge for a bottle of water. She passed one to him.

"Thanks." He placed it on the counter and continued spreading peanut butter on one slice of bread.

Without a word, she took her lunch to the family room.

"I guess I'm in for the silent treatment," he said to Bob, who had hesitated before following her.

He slapped the two slices of bread together and grabbed his water, then took the same path she had taken. She stood at the front window peeking through the blinds. Her sandwich and water had been abandoned on the coffee table.

"It's snowing again."

She said this as if she were speaking to herself rather than to anyone in particular. He joined her at the window and leaned his head to the right far enough to see through the two slats she had parted. She drew away the slightest bit.

"Looks like the meteorologist got it right for once." Snow had been in the forecast, but in this part of the country there was rarely a follow-through.

She released the slats and walked back to the sofa. It was a large L-shaped one. He settled on the opposite end from her. He didn't need a crystal ball to tell him she wasn't interested in having him too close.

"You worried about tomorrow?" He tore off a bite of the sandwich and chewed as he waited for her response.

"Not really." She nibbled her sandwich, eating like a bird.

"I've already mapped out a route." He'd been thinking about it since the command performance was issued. There was little likelihood of them being discovered en route with the precautions he had outlined. There was always the risk that their travel plans could be leaked. It had happened before. To ensure that didn't happen again, he had not provided the route he intended to take to anyone. Better to be safe than sorry.

"I'm not worried," she said in case he hadn't gotten it the first time.

She chewed and swallowed, chewed and swallowed. Clearly she wasn't enjoying the food. He figured if he hadn't mentioned that they should eat, she wouldn't have bothered. It was his job to keep her safe and to ensure she was ready to testify at trial on Thursday. To that end, his duties included seeing that she ate, slept and behaved responsibly.

"If you have any questions about how things will go on Thursday, I can probably answer them." She hadn't asked a single question during the conference call.

"I don't have any questions." She drank more of her water and wadded the napkin she'd used for a plate.

"Good." He finished his sandwich and chugged the rest of his water.

The silence was deafening. He considered going back to the kitchen and making coffee, but the enthusiasm just wasn't there. There were things he wanted to ask...to say, but none of it would come out the way he wanted. He was too angry about what she had done. *Angry* might not be the right word. He wasn't exactly angry. He was disappointed. The crazy part was he had no right to feel either way.

As she had so accurately pointed out, he'd been the one to leave.

No point going down that path again.

He stood and returned to the kitchen. Tossed his trash and made a pot of coffee. The silence was a lot easier to tolerate if he found some way to occupy himself.

The scent of fresh-brewed coffee filled the air, and he relaxed marginally. Today and tonight were going to pass painstakingly slowly. They had both said plenty, maybe too much on some subjects. There was nothing else to discuss.

Words weren't going to change deeds.

What was done was done.

"I do have one question."

Surprised that she had walked into the room without him detecting her presence, he turned to face her. "What might that be?"

"The day we go to trial, will you be wearing a bulletproof vest?"

So they were back to his safety, were they? "I've already told you there's no reason for you to worry about me. I know how to do this."

She stared at him, unblinking, determined. "You asked me if I had any questions. That's my question."

"Yes. And so will you."

Apparently satisfied with his answer, she turned and walked away.

Was it possible that she was actually that worried about him?

He shook his head. Made no sense.

Chapter Seven

The snow had stopped, leaving enough to cover the grass and adorn the trees and rooftop. Ali had always liked snow, but growing up in Georgia she had rarely seen it outside Christmas movie marathons. On the rare occasion it did snow, it was a given that it wouldn't last long. Vivid memories of both her parents romping in the snow with her when she was a child assaulted her, took her breath.

Bob nudged her with his nose, and she smiled down at him. "Sorry, boy, I was lost in thought."

Somewhere close by, Jax would be trailing her. There wasn't really any place to go unless she wanted to attempt climbing higher up the mountain. The edge of the tree line provided a sweeping view of the valley below. Even the faded asphalt far below that zigzagged through the valley was covered in snow. Not a single vehicle had driven along that road since their arrival. She hoped they would be safe here until the day after tomorrow, when they headed to Atlanta for the trial.

According to the conference call this morning, they were booked under aliases on a commercial flight from Huntsville, Alabama, to Atlanta. The airport in Huntsville was less than an hour away. Jax had said they would leave early Wednesday morning and, per the usual protocol, take back roads until they had no other choice.

When this began, her attorney had mentioned to her the possibility that dedicated followers of old man Armone might haunt her for many years after his incarceration. Assuming she survived to testify and all went as expected during the trial. There was always the chance, she supposed, that a jury could be intimidated or bought off.

But no one was going to let a man who shot his own son get away with it. Right?

Ali hugged her jacket tighter around her and turned back toward the house. Jax lingered a few yards behind. His gaze caught hers briefly as she walked past him. She had been thinking that it might be best to try and make amends of some sort. If she didn't live through this, the idea of him spending the rest of his life harboring this resentment he felt toward her was more than she wanted to take to her grave.

He was the one who'd left, and in her mind he owed her the apology, explanation, whatever. Not vice versa. But he didn't see it that way. All he saw were the facts. She had married a ruthless criminal. Had stayed married to him for five years until he was murdered. Admittedly, that didn't look so great.

But there were so many things he didn't know. Things she could not bear to tell anyone beyond the official statement she had given over the course of a week when this thing began.

Rather shortsightedly, she had walked into that FBI office in Kentucky and identified herself. No further explanation had been needed. Immediately, the powers that be were gathered into conference rooms across the southeast and decisions were made. She was interviewed over and over for weeks. Finally when a course of action was decided upon, she was whisked away into hiding to await trial.

There had been no fanfare, no sense of adventure or excitement. Just more loneliness. The deep, sad loneliness she had felt for years by that point. At least the physical pain had stopped.

Oddly, the physical pain was the only aspect of those last three years of her marriage that reminded her she was still alive. She had felt dead most of the time. A body floating through time. The numbness that had overtaken her life had been profound— except for the physical pain he wielded. Sometimes she even looked forward to the moments when the pain reminded her that her heart was still beating.

She wasn't sure what a psychiatrist would say about that. Most likely she didn't want to know.

Stamping the snow from her shoes at the back door, she smiled as Bob shook himself, as well.

"Come on, boy."

They went inside, and Jax followed. She peeled

off her jacket and hung it in the mudroom before continuing on into the kitchen. Rubbing her hands together, she went in search of a treat for Bob. She found a small bag of jerky that was still in date.

Bob shifted from paw to paw with excitement as she opened the bag. She gave him a piece, and he sauntered off to pile up in front of the fireplace. Bob liked being near the heat and maybe the crackle of the logs. Then again, it didn't take a lot to make him happy. The occasional scratch behind the ears, walks and food.

In her opinion, he had the right idea. She longed for simple again.

Finally, she turned to face the man watching her. "We need to talk."

He lifted one shoulder and let it drop. "Talk."

"Can we go in the other room and sit while we talk?" No matter that the sun was dropping, light poured into the kitchen's western-facing windows. She didn't want to have this discussion in such unforgiving light.

He gestured to the other room. "After you."

She sat in a chair near where Bob lay. The fire had died down a little while they were out walking. Jax added a couple more logs to fuel the flames. He settled on the sofa, which allowed him to stare directly at her.

"Just so you know," he said before she could begin, "you don't owe me an explanation. You're right. I left. You had every right to move on with your life as you saw fit."

His face told her he didn't really see it that way.

"After you left for Seattle, I focused on my classes. It was lonely and I was heartbroken."

He started to speak but she held up a hand to stop him.

"I was young. I hadn't even turned twenty-two yet. You were my first love and, of course, I was devastated. I was a bit of a late bloomer, so I hadn't experienced that kind of intense relationship before." She swallowed, mustered the courage to say the rest. "It wasn't your fault that I had been so sheltered until then."

She waited to see if he had anything to say. When he didn't, she moved on.

"For the next two years, I hung on to the idea that you would be back." She laughed softly. "I was confident you loved me just as much as I loved you and that you'd come back and all would be well again."

His expression changed then. The defensive face melted into something softer, something aching.

"Then my father became ill, and I had to leave school to take care of him. I only had two semesters left, but there was no putting off going home. He was very, very sick."

She fell quiet for a moment, remembering those pain-filled days. Her father was the only family she'd had left. Saying goodbye to him had been so very difficult.

"Before he died, he made me promise that I would go back and finish school. So I did. I left everything at the farm just as it was and completed my final semesters. By that time I felt as if I could go back and pack things up. Do what I had to do. It took a couple of months, but I got it done. The farm sold practically before I could put it on the market. I decided I wanted to go someplace where I could disappear into the energy and excitement. Atlanta felt like the place."

"You went to work for Clayton and Ross, and the rest is history," he said, the defensive face and tone back in full swing.

"I had no idea the accounting firm had anything to do with the Armone family." She shrugged. "I had no idea who the Armone family was. The firm offered a very competitive salary plus a bonus. They would pay for my master's. It was a win-win situation. I found a small apartment and even bought a new car with part of the money from the farm." She shook her head. "I was so happy. It felt like a fresh beginning. I had been lonely and sad for so long."

Jax stood. "Then what? Let me guess. Armone came in and swept you off your feet. You had no idea who he was. Thought he was a knight in shining armor." He walked over to where she sat and crouched down to her eye level. "But you stayed married to him for five years. *Five years*. Nearly two thousand days and nights. You had to have figured out who he was way before that much time elapsed. But you stayed." He pushed to his feet. "You're doing the right thing now, and that's great. I'm here for you. But for far too long, you pretended you had no idea who the man you were crawling into bed with every night was."

Fury and regret made her lips tremble. "There are things you don't know."

He planted his hands on his hips. "Tell me."

She shook her head. She couldn't tell him those things. Ever. The idea of how he would look at her was too painful. She couldn't bear it. Let him think what he would. She had tried to make things right between them.

"I guess there's nothing else to say."

With that pointed announcement, he walked away.

That was the thing with Jax. He always walked away.

THE SUN HAD DISAPPEARED, and darkness had settled over the landscape. The thin layer of snow reflected the light from the moon. Jax had spent the evening checking the perimeter and ensuring all was locked up tight.

Ali's words about being sad and lonely kept echoing in his brain. He didn't want to feel the regret that had crowded into his chest. She had made her own decisions. Yes, he was the one to leave. But he'd been young, damn it. A fool. And yes, it took him a long time to see that fact, and by then it was too late.

Why did she feel compelled to keep trying to make him understand?

He didn't understand. He didn't want to understand. He wanted to keep an emotional distance between them, because he didn't want to feel what he was feeling.

Damn it.

She had said there were things he didn't know.

Probably just another excuse. She'd had everything she wanted. Money, power, prestige. Who knows what prompted her to decide to testify against the old man? Maybe she was afraid she would be next after he executed his own son.

Or maybe she and the old man had something going on.

He closed his eyes. Hated himself for even thinking such a thing. Anger, resentment, regret—all those emotions were driving him right now. He had to work through this. To keep his head clear.

Brannigan had mentioned the pain she had endured. Did that have something to do with the part she refused to share with him?

Before going back in the house, he put through a call to Holloway.

"Everything okay?" The worry in the other marshal's voice was palpable.

"Yeah. Everything's fine."

"You don't sound fine."

Holloway knew him well enough to hear the doubt in his voice.

"I need to see the entire file." A part of him wanted to argue with his own words. That part of his instincts that warned he would regret knowing nudged him. He ignored it. He had to know the whole story.

Holloway didn't respond for a bit. Finally, he said, "If she wants—"

"She's not going to tell me," Jax said, cutting him off. "Holloway, I wouldn't ask if it wasn't necessary. If Brannigan can be briefed on the part I don't know, I can, as well. I need to get my head screwed on right with this."

More of that lingering silence.

"You said this wouldn't be a problem. Tell me now if you were wrong. I don't want Ali at even more risk because you can't get beyond the past. As for what I shared with Brannigan, that was necessary. I needed his input."

"I can handle her security," Jax argued. "I just need to know the rest so I can get…" He exhaled a big breath. No use lying to the man. He would see through it. "I need to get my personal feelings sorted out, and I can't do that until I understand what she isn't telling me."

"This is her life, Stevens. She doesn't have to tell you anything."

"You know I'll hear it at trial," Jax reminded him. "Better for me to know now and be prepared."

Holloway was the one letting go of a sigh now. "You're right. Maybe I should have given you the whole story to begin with. But understand, this is intensely personal. You don't need to know in order to do your job."

He was aware that Holloway was only agreeing to indulge his personal needs.

"I don't want to go into this on the phone. I'll make sure you see the entire file tomorrow while you're in Nashville for the teleconference. There's a video you need to see. I think that will take care of whatever is nagging at you."

"All right." He could wait until tomorrow. "I appreciate it, Holloway."

"You may change your mind when you see the video."

His gut tightened. "Better to know the whole truth," he argued.

"Sometimes maybe not," Holloway countered. "Just keep her safe, Stevens. This might sound lame, but if anyone has ever needed a real-life hero, it's this woman."

The call ended, and Jax stared at the house. Ali had been standing at the window watching him, but she wasn't there now.

He'd said too much. Every time they talked about the past, his anger got the better of him. Not once in his adult life had he had this problem with anyone else. He'd always been easygoing, nonjudgmental.

But he couldn't maintain his objectivity in her presence.

This was the real problem. He still had feelings for her, and it drove him crazy.

He didn't want to feel any of this. He just wanted to do his job.

Inside the back door, he locked up and removed his jacket. Maybe he should make another pot of coffee and see if she would open up to him. Why hear the truth from a stranger when she was right here?

He emptied the carafe, rinsed away the old grounds from the brew basket and prepared a fresh pot. When it started to brew, he went in search of her. She'd already shut herself and Bob up in her room. He stood outside her closed door and tried to think of something to say.

Finally he shook his head. Tomorrow would just have to be soon enough to hear the rest of her story.

Ali stood at the door, her hands pressed to the cool wooden surface. She closed her eyes and laid her cheek there. As much as she wanted his forgiveness, his understanding, she could not tell him the details of her marriage.

It was too painful. She couldn't bear to see the pity in his eyes.

When this was over, he would go on his way, and she would go hers. Vying for his understanding was a selfish luxury that was not necessary to her continued existence. She would get over the hurt. It wouldn't be the first time she'd had her heart fracture over Jaxson Stevens.

He moved away from the door. She felt his withdrawal more than heard it. She moved away, as well.

It was only eight o'clock. Going to bed this early was a little ridiculous, but it was safer than allowing that little voice in her head to goad her into telling him the whole story.

What he didn't know wouldn't hurt him or change what he was assigned to do. It would, however, devastate her.

In hindsight, there were parts she wished she hadn't shared in those initial interviews. But she had been desperate, vulnerable. The story of her marriage to Harrison Armone had poured out of her like a poison her body had needed to expel. Each time she fell silent, the interviewer was there, prodding her for more. No one would ever hear those parts, the agents had promised.

As time moved on, she had slowly but surely been informed that it might become necessary to use those details as proof of her motivation for coming forward. The fear, the humiliation and endless abuse she suffered could be an incredible asset for setting the tone for the jury.

Ali was a victim, and the jurors needed to see that victim. They needed to feel her pain.

She paced the room. Keeping Jax out of the courtroom was likely impossible. He would hear all the gory details, and there was nothing she could do to prevent it. But at least she wouldn't have to look at him. She would focus on the man questioning her.

As much as she dreaded that part of the questioning, she would do whatever necessary to see that the bastard went away. He could not be allowed to get away with all that he and his son had done.

It was time he paid.

She climbed onto the bed and closed her eyes. After all she had endured, it would be almost worth it to see the look on his face when the jury announced, "Guilty."

Chapter Eight

Two days until trial

Tuesday, February 4

Ali pulled on her jacket and finished off her second cup of coffee. She stared out the window over the sink. Thin patches of snow lingered here and there, but it would be gone by midday with the subtle rise in temperature. The interstate to Nashville wouldn't be a problem either way, but some of the back roads might still be icy this morning.

Jax had said back roads would be the word of the day. The only person who knew their exact route was Marshal Holloway, and even he didn't know the turn-by-turn details. Both she and Jax trusted him implicitly. They'd spoken this morning. She was so thankful he had been released from the hospital late yesterday. He was still on leave because of his injuries, but he was healing. Ali appreciated all that he had done for her this past six months. The first marshal assigned to her hadn't been so friendly. She had gotten the impression he had considered her a lesser life form. But he had done his job and gotten her out of danger when the time came.

"You ready?"

She turned to the man who had spoken. They hadn't said a word to each other since that unpleasant exchange late yesterday. Not even good morning.

He'd gone outside and checked his SUV. Not that he'd told her what he planned to do when he walked out the door. She'd watched from a window. He'd gone over the vehicle very carefully. Surely if anyone who had intended to do harm had found their location, they would have burst into the cabin and done so last night. Then again, she supposed it was better to be safe than sorry.

When he'd finished his inspection, she was back in the kitchen pulling on her jacket. She decided not to worry about her purse. All she needed was her driver's license and lip moisturizer. Those she carried in her left jacket pocket. The emergency cell phone Holloway had given her was in the other pocket.

"I am," she said in answer to his question. She rinsed her cup and placed it on the counter before turning to face him.

"We should get started just in case we run into any closed roads."

She crouched down and gave Bob a hug. "You take care of the place while we're gone."

His tail wagged, and she gave him a scratch on the head as she stood. She followed Jax out the front door and to his SUV. A minute later they were rolling down the treacherous road that led back down to the paved one below. Ali found herself holding her breath more than once.

Once they were on the paved road and moving along at a faster speed, she relaxed. She'd pinned her hair up and back in a makeshift twist this morning. She rarely wore it that way, but it was important not to look like her usual self.

No matter that she had prepared for the trial, trepidation was building inside her. She tried to tamp it down, but there was no holding it back. In forty-eight hours, she would have the opportunity to tell the world just how evil the Armone family was. Truly, viciously evil. She wanted to do this. Nothing outside of a bullet to her brain would stop her.

But that didn't mean she wasn't scared.

Of course, she said this to no one.

Jax rolled to a stop at the Highway 64 intersection. He reached across to the glove box, and she found herself holding her breath again. He popped it open and pulled out a pair of sunglasses.

"Put these on."

She accepted the eyewear and slid it into place. "Thank you."

The half hour that followed was thick with tension and silence. He drove around, bypassing Winchester proper. The road they were on now felt like a tunnel through a dense wood. Traffic was light. School buses were already off the roads. The other time she'd gone to Nashville, it had only taken ninety or so minutes but Marshal Holloway had taken the interstate. This would likely take a lot more time. But they had plenty.

She closed her eyes and allowed his scent to envelop her. After ten years how was it she could recall the scent of him so precisely? Whatever aftershave he wore, it was subtle. Earthy like amber, with the slightest hint of something sweet like honey. She'd loved the smell and taste of his skin. They had been so young—all they wanted to do was get lost in each other.

He was her first love, her first in every way.

Her eyes opened, and she forced away the memories. Not a good idea to get lost in those.

"Do you have any questions or concerns about today?"

She dared to turn her head to study his profile. Those lean, angular features tugged at her. The swell of his lips, the straightness of his nose. High cheekbones. His thick hair fell over his forehead. How many times had she seen that face in her dreams?

She blinked, faced forward. What was wrong with her this morning? "No."

He was doing his job, not trying to make conversation. He had made that very clear last night.

Could she blame him for not understanding how she came to be Mrs. Harrison Armone? Not really.

I guess you had to be there.

Last night she had decided not to pursue trying to make him understand. This was her burden to carry. The idea of him feeling the way he did about her forevermore was painful, but she had no power to control his feelings. She could only control her own, and she had spent far too much time as a prisoner to someone else's desires and demands. She would not be a prisoner any longer.

"We'll stop just before we arrive in Nashville for a break."

He didn't ask if she was good with that, simply made the statement. To her way of thinking, a response was not required.

She closed her eyes and rested her head against the seat.

It was time to think about the future. For months she had feared she wouldn't have a future. Finally she could see the tiniest flicker of light at the end of the tunnel. Why not make a plan just in case she did survive?

THE TELECONFERENCE WAS scheduled in the Estes Ke- fauver Federal Building on Ninth Avenue South, only steps from Broadway and countless legendary coun- try music spots, like the Ryman Auditorium and the Country Music Hall of Fame.

Rather than park in the designated parking area, Jax drove over a street and parked in the lot of a huge church. From there he called an Uber that would take them right up to the door. Considering only half a dozen people—people he knew—were aware of this meeting, he hoped he didn't have to worry about a leak, but he wasn't taking the risk.

Ali had answered the few questions he had when they started out, but she hadn't said a word otherwise. He'd said too much last night. That he'd felt tremendously guilty only minutes later made no difference, since he'd opted not to apologize. In forty-eight hours, this assignment would be over. He could manage two more days without running his mouth off again.

He'd received the color and make of the vehicle as well as a picture of the driver when he made the reservation, so he spotted the tan-colored sedan when it turned into the parking lot. He allowed the driver to go past their position before getting out. Since he drove slowly, Jax was able to identify him.

"That's our ride. Don't get out until I'm at your door."

He climbed out and went around to the passenger side of the car. After surveying the area, he opened her door and she emerged. He hit the lock button for his SUV and waved down the Uber driver.

Once they were in the sedan, Jax leaned forward and said, "We've changed our mind about where we want to go."

In the rearview mirror, Jax watched the guy's eyebrows lift in question.

"Estes Kefauver Federal Building. Ninth Avenue entrance." He passed the man a fifty.

The driver shrugged. "Works for me."

The walk would have only been two blocks, but that wasn't the point. The point was to maintain some semblance of cover until they reached the entrance.

Jax scanned the street in both directions, the sidewalks. He watched to ensure no vehicles were braking near where they wanted to get out. All they had to do was get out of the car on the passenger side and hustle across fifteen or so feet of sidewalk.

When the car stopped the driver asked, "You need an updated receipt?"

"No, thanks." Jax opened the door and climbed out.

He scanned the street and sidewalk again and then motioned for Ali to get out, as well. Once she was out of the car, he shoved the door shut and rushed her across the span of sidewalk and through the doors.

Once they were beyond the security checkpoint, he relaxed. The third floor was their destination. Ali stopped him before they reached the elevators.

"I'd like to find the ladies' room."

He nodded. "This way."

A short corridor right off the lobby led to the restrooms. He stopped her before she pushed through the door.

"I need to check it out first."

She started to argue but then shook her head.

Keeping her close to his side, he pushed the door open and shouted, "Hello! Anyone in here?"

He waited three beats, and when no one responded, he walked inside with Ali.

"You shouldn't be in here," she said.

He held up his hand. "As soon as I know there's no one else in here, I'll get out of your way."

One by one he checked the stalls. Looked all the way around the room. Clear.

"I'll be right outside."

She nodded and watched until he was out the door. He stationed himself directly in front of it to ensure no one else went inside until Ali was finished.

After they'd gone through security, he noticed that she looked a little pale. She was more nervous than she wanted him to know. Understandable.

She wore jeans as she had every day since he arrived, but today she wore a pink sweater instead of the usual sweatshirt. The color made her look even more vulnerable. He doubted that had been her goal. Her wardrobe was limited, but he had seen a black skirt and jacket in a hanging bag. For court, he assumed.

He shifted his weight to the other foot and wondered what was taking so long. Just when he'd decided maybe he'd poke his head in and check on her, the door opened with a hydraulic *whoosh*.

They continued to the bank of elevators. He moved in front of her as an elevator opened. Two people emerged, and only when he ensured the car was empty did they walk through those doors. He selected the floor and hoped the elevator didn't stop on two.

When the elevator stopped on three, she looked at him. "Will you be in the room?"

"Only long enough to ensure you're settled, and then I have some things to take care of across the hall. But I won't be more than a few steps away."

She nodded, her expression clearly relieved.

AUSA Knowles and his assistant waited in the conference room, along with Tom Phillips, another of the marshals assigned to Nashville, and FBI special agents Willis and Kurtz. These were all people Jax knew well.

Introductions were made, and the teleconference began. Once Ali's attorney and the AUSA from Atlanta were online, Jax slipped out and went across the hall. Agent Kurtz followed. He had agreed to prepare the file and accompanying videotaped interview for Jax's perusal.

"Good to see you, Stevens." Kurtz said as he opened the laptop on the table. "How's Holloway?"

"He's doing better," Jax said, "but he'll be out of commission for a while yet."

Kurtz pointed to the screen. "This file contains all the case documents. This one has the video interview. I'll be across the hall if you need anything."

Jax thanked him and turned his attention to the laptop. The room was a small meeting area designed for separate discussion when the need arose during a larger meeting across the hall.

First, he skimmed the documents. A good deal of the file was compilations of the material gathered over decades regarding the suspected activities of the Armone family. He read page after page of how Ali had come to know Harrison Armone and when they had married. He hadn't known the more intimate details, like the fact that he'd run into her in the lobby at the firm where she worked and then he'd shown up at her office every day until she agreed to have dinner with him.

The words sickened him. He kept seeing that bastard touching her. He closed his eyes and shook his head. If he didn't know better, he would think he'd just gotten jealous reading about some other guy with Ali.

No way.

This was something else altogether. He just couldn't name what it was.

He plowed through the fairy-tale first year. Travel, expensive jewelry, lavish shopping sprees. The castle of a home.

He cleared his throat of the bile that threatened.

Then the day a covolunteer had asked the question that changed her life.

You're married to Harrison Armone?

On that day, she opened her eyes.

Her first mistake had been discussing the question with her husband.

The evidence and the terror started to build until there was no way for her to pretend. She had tried to keep up the pretense but Armone had felt the change…saw it in her eyes…felt it in her touch.

The fairy tale was over.

Then I became his prisoner.

The statement startled Jax. He read it three times before moving on.

The file then referenced the videotaped interview. It was standard procedure to record statements. For the purposes of a jury trial, it was always better to have a living, breathing witness, but in the event something went wrong, the video could make the necessary difference.

Jax closed the folder and moved on to the one containing the video. He double clicked the icon dated just over nine months ago and waited. The screen opened, and Ali came into focus. The interviewer instructed her to recite her name and other pertinent information. She did this. He was impressed with how calm and strong she looked as she spoke. She recited a lengthy monologue that basically recounted what he had read in the file.

He stretched his back and repositioned himself. His body felt as if he'd been sitting here for hours when it had only been forty or so minutes.

"How was Mr. Armone able to keep you prisoner?" the interviewer asked. "Did he lock you in a room? Shackle you in some way? The jury needs to understand why you continued to live with a man like Armone and why you didn't come forward sooner."

Jax would like to understand that, as well.

Ali's chest rose with a deep breath. She moistened her lips. "He told me what he would do if I ever left him."

"What did he tell you he would do?"

Another big breath. "He said he would kill me and bury parts of me all over the city."

Jax felt his shoulders tense.

"How could you be sure his threat was real? Had you seen him murder anyone?"

She shook her head.

"You'll need to voice your answers," the interviewer reminded.

"No. Not then. I had overheard phone calls about taking care of situations and cleaning up problems. But he was very careful what he said over the phone. It was the discussions between him and his father that warned me I shouldn't doubt what he was capable of. They would drink and smoke cigars once a week in my—in Harrison's study. I started taking every opportunity possible to listen in."

"Did you learn anything specific?"

One by one, she listed names and dates of "fixes" and "cleanups." Jax didn't need to refer to the file to know those were dates that major power shifts occurred. Bodies showed up. New people took over in the Armone operation.

The interviewer referenced a document that would

be listed into evidence. The document was a time-line that laid out the murders that occurred on the dates she recited.

"You were gathering this evidence for a reason?" he asked.

"Yes. I wanted to have enough for the FBI to arrest him and his father."

"Again, I ask, how did he keep you from leaving for so long?"

She blinked, looked away from the camera for a moment before answering. Jax watched her eyes, saw the fear mingling with the determination.

"In the beginning, when he wasn't home, I was forced to spend part of the day shackled in my room. Whenever I was allowed to leave the room, one of his men accompanied me. To the bathroom, when I showered. Anywhere I went—to the dentist, shopping, whatever, I was escorted. I was never out of his sight. Never."

"But you attempted to escape, did you not?"

She nodded. "The first man, Tate. I'm not sure whether that was his first name or his last." She stared at her hands a moment. "Harrison had a big dinner party coming up. I told him I needed to go to the spa for my hair and nails. He ordered Tate to take me there and shopping for something new to wear. At the spa, when I went back to change into a robe was the first time Tate had not followed me into a changing room. He got a call on his cell. I guess he was distracted."

"What did you do?"

"I went out the back and ran."

She stared at her hands again.

"But he found you."

"Tate caught up with me. He took me back home and called Harrison. He came home immediately. I was terrified."

"What did he do?"

She lifted her gaze and looked directly into the camera. "He shot Tate right in front of me. Told me his death was on me." She swallowed hard. "Then everything got worse."

"Worse? He'd just killed a man in front of you. What could be worse?"

Her eyes glittered with emotion. "There are worse things than dying."

She dropped her gaze for a moment.

"The jury will need to understand what that means, Ms. Armone."

Jax's gut tightened at hearing her called that. He rubbed at the back of his neck. Sweat had popped out on his skin.

"He punished me severely for forcing him to kill an old friend."

Jax drew slightly away from the screen.

"Punished you how?"

"He withheld food. Water. Kept me shackled naked in my room for days with the lights off and the blinds closed tight. Once he felt I had been suf-ficiently punished for trying to run away, he removed the shackle and told me he had decided on new rules."

The silence throbbed for too many seconds.

Every muscle in Jax's body had grown rigid with tension.

"He told me what to wear. Clothes, makeup. Everything. How to walk. When to speak. When to eat. If I made a mistake, he…"

She stared at her hands as she went on. "He tortured me."

Those three words stabbed deep into Jax. He wanted to push away from the table. To shut off the volume. But he had to keep listening. He had to know the rest.

"Sometimes he used a leather whip. The number of lashes I received was determined by the severity of my mistake. Did I say the wrong thing or wear the wrong perfume?

"Over the course of the next two years, I had a dislocated shoulder. A fractured arm. Two concussions and a series of burns." Her breath caught, yet somehow she managed to go on. "There were other, more intimate methods of inflicting pain he utilized, depending upon my infraction."

Jax stared at the face on the screen. It hurt to breathe. The crushing sensation against his chest was unbearable. Why hadn't she told him any of this?

Why the hell hadn't Holloway told him?

"Were you taken for medical attention?"

"His personal physician always came and attended

to my injuries." A single tear rolled past her lashes and slid down her cheek.

"This was a very painful time for you."

"Yes." She flinched. "But I never cried."

She shook her head. "I would have died before I let him see my pain. He'd already taken my pride, my hopes and dreams. I wouldn't allow him to have anything else."

"On May 2 of last year, you witnessed one last travesty. Describe that event for the jury."

"My father-in-law, Harrison Sr., came for his weekly visit. He and Harrison went to his study for the usual evening of cigars and scotch. I recognized an added layer of tension between the two."

"Was there anyone else in the house?"

"Always. But Harrison had sent them outside. He and his father preferred complete privacy."

"Did you overhear anything different this night?"

"I didn't have to try and overhear this time. Mr. Armone asked me to join them. He told me to stand by the window so he could look at me as he and Harrison spoke. I was very uncomfortable. Harrison only laughed. I suppose he had bragged to his father about how he was punishing me."

She paused to draw in a deep breath.

"Mr. Armone suddenly announced that he was aware of what Harrison was doing—attempting to take over the business. Harrison denied the allegation. He stood and paced the room, ranting about how someone was only trying to cause trouble between them. Mr. Armone ordered him to sit. He did as his father said. Then Mr. Armone circled him as if considering what to say next. He paused, drew a handgun from his jacket and fired a single shot into the back of his son's head. Harrison slumped forward in his chair."

"What did you do?"

"Nothing." She blinked. "I stood there the way I'd been told."

Outrage burst inside Jax, so powerful that he couldn't stay seated. He pushed to his feet, his hands searching for a place to land.

"What happened next?"

"Mr. Armone looked at me and told me that now I belonged to him."

Jax hit Pause, his gut pulsing with the need to vomit up the sick details he'd just heard. He stared at her face…at her pale skin, her weary blue eyes.

He had been wrong. Dead wrong.

The one thing he knew for an absolutely certainty was that the bastard would never get his hands on Ali again.

He'd have to go through Jax to get to her, and that was not going to happen.

Chapter Nine

"Everything go okay?"

Jax asked even though he was aware that it had. He'd caught the last fifteen minutes of the meeting. Ali had sounded strong and calm. The AUSAs had sounded satisfied that she was ready for trial.

The two of them had left the building the same way they arrived. He'd had the driver circle the lot where his SUV was parked three times before he stopped. During those slow circles, he had carefully surveyed their surroundings as well as his SUV. When the other car had driven away, he'd checked the SUV more closely before they loaded up.

For the first fifty or so miles, she hadn't spoken and he hadn't, either. On some level he had known if he said anything he would say too much. The things he'd read…the words she had said in that video had ripped him apart inside. A whole new guilt had settled on him then. It was his fault this had happened. If he hadn't left…if he had stayed, she would never have gone to Atlanta and met the SOB.

But he hadn't stayed. He'd left her alone. He hadn't even come back when he'd learned her father had passed away. It was days after his funeral when Jax discovered that he'd died. Why hadn't he come back then? There had been nothing left holding her in Georgia at that point.

Pride. Plain and simple. He had practically begged her to go with him ten years ago, and she'd said no. He wasn't going to ask again. This time she would have to make the decision on her own. What a fool he'd been. He should have realized she was devastated by the loss. Overwhelmed with settling her father's estate. He should have come back, been supportive. Then if she hadn't mentioned wanting to try again with him, he would know he had done all he could do. He would have done the right thing.

Too late now.

His pride had kept him away, and the longer he'd stayed away the easier it had become.

"Yes," she said in answer to his question. "It was basically the same as the last conference call. Nothing I wasn't expecting."

"Good."

He clenched his jaw before words he couldn't say burst out. If he said he was sorry, she would ask about what, and then he would have to tell her something. Anything he said would likely lead her to understand that he had seen the video. He was in hell. Trapped in this place where he now knew the truth but couldn't tell her. She would feel humiliated and betrayed. He didn't want to add to the pain she had already suffered.

What he wanted was to kill Harrison Armone Jr., except the bastard's father had already done that. His gut clenched at the idea that the old man had dared to kill his own son and then assume he could claim his widow for his own.

"You want to stop for food?" He hadn't intended to stop, but he was confident they were in the clear. He had taken a different route, still back roads, but not the same ones they had used on the drive up.

"I'd just like to get back to Bob." She turned, allowed her gaze to meet his but only briefly. "If you don't mind."

"No problem. We should reach Huntland in about thirty minutes."

The silence closed in on them again. He didn't attempt to restart a conversation. Maybe later.

He had to find a way to say the words burgeoning in his chest. He owed her an apology. He needed her to understand that he hadn't meant to...

What?

Leave her vulnerable? Be a coward?

That was the real problem. He'd blamed her for not choosing him over everything else in her life when the truth was he had known she wouldn't desert her father. He had been a coward. She had consumed his entire existence. He hadn't been able to think of anything but her. They had both been so young.

He'd needed time.

But he'd taken too long.

It was far too late to make that right now.

ALI WAS GRATEFUL when they started the precarious climb up that narrow mountain road. Not really a road, she decided. Just a really long, infinitely tight driveway. The snow was gone now. But the sun was slipping downward and the temperature was dropping. This gravel and dirt road would be truly treacherous with a layer of ice on it. The drop-off on the cliff side provided no leeway for mistakes.

At the top of the rise, the house came into view. No matter that it was still daylight, the gloom that hung from the darkening sky warned that more snow might just show up. The last few minutes of the trip, she hadn't been able to bear the silence any longer, so she'd turned on the radio. When the hour rolled around, the local news had included a weather forecast. The meteorologist mentioned the possibility of another dusting of snow. Probably not more than an inch.

Jax parked and got out, locking her in until he was certain the house was clear. Per the usual protocol, she waited while he had a look around. He checked the front door and started around the house. He would make a complete circle and then take her inside.

She glanced toward the woods. It would be dark soon. It had been a long day. She didn't like reviewing the horrors of the past five years, but it was necessary to ensure her testimony went smoothly. It wasn't like she would ever forget a single moment of the horror—not if she lived a thousand years.

Movement at her door made her jump.

Jax.

She pressed a hand to her throat, her heart threatening to burst out of her chest, then reached for the door.

"Get down," he ordered through the glass. "Stay down until I tell you otherwise."

Fear pulsing through her, she scrambled to the floorboard, hunkered down to make herself as small as possible.

She kept her eye on the window of her door and reminded herself to breathe. The idea that any second she might hear gunfire seared through her. Jax could be killed. She would be next.

What about Bob?

What felt like long minutes later but was likely only a few, Jax appeared at her door once more. This time he opened it and extended his hand to help her out.

"What happened?" She struggled to ease her hips between the seat and the dash.

"The back door was standing open."

That fear that had twisted deep inside her expanded now. "Where's Bob?"

"He's not inside."

Ali rushed to the house. She started to call his name the instant she was through the door. Jax had told her he wasn't in the house, but she needed to see for herself. She bounded up the stairs and checked the bedrooms.

No Bob.

Jax waited for her at the bottom of the stairs.

"We have to find him." She shook her head. "Why would someone break in and take him?"

His eyes told her the answer without him having to say a word.

"No." She shook her head.

"Let's not go there just yet," he said gently, more gently than he had spoken to her since he walked back into her life. "I checked the lock. It doesn't stay latched every time, so it may not have been an intruder. I locked and unlocked it several times. If the latch doesn't catch properly, it doesn't lock. Bob may have swiped past it and caused it to open. Maybe the house has settled and the door is no longer square in its frame." He pushed it to and showed her how the door drifted open on its own when the lock wasn't fully engaged.

Her heart slowed to a more normal rate. "So he's probably out there in the woods somewhere." Her gaze sought his. "Lost. It's going to be cold tonight. We have to find him."

"We'll look for him. Let me get the flashlight from my SUV just in case it gets dark on us before we find him."

"Thank you."

She didn't know why he had suddenly started to

be so nice to her, but she didn't care as long as he helped her find Bob.

They walked around the perimeter of the property and called the dog's name. The third or fourth time, they got a response. Bob started to bark.

Ali scanned the tree line. "Where is that coming from?"

They moved faster now, calling out to him to prod him to bark again.

"This way," Jax said as he turned and hurried toward the side of the property that overlooked the valley below.

Ali's heart dropped into her stomach. If he was on that side...

The barking was louder now.

Jax called out to him, and Bob barked as if he understood they needed to follow the sound.

Please let him be okay.

The cold had cut through her clothes and invaded her bones. Her fingers felt numb, but she didn't care. They had to find him.

At the edge of the cliff, Ali stood, her heart pounding as she stared into the gloom enveloping the trees and brush that covered the mountainside.

His bark was more enthusiastic now. He was close, and he recognized their nearness.

"Where are you, boy?"

"I can't see him," Jax muttered, roving his flashlight over the area below them.

"I need to climb down," she said, worry clawing

at her. It was the only way to find him. Obviously he was trapped somehow. Or possibly injured. Otherwise he would have run to them by now.

"You stay put," he ordered. "I'll go down."

He removed the weapon from his shoulder holster and handed it to her, butt first. "Don't hesitate to use it. Holloway says you're a good shot."

Ali nodded. She couldn't have spoken if her life depended upon it. She turned around a dozen times, checking behind her, while Jax disappeared below. Bob's bark had grown frantic.

Her body started to shake from the cold and maybe from the fear. Adrenaline or something.

Finally, she heard Jax coming back up.

Even in the darkness she spotted the big old black lab in his arms. She rushed to help him.

"We have to get him to a vet," Jax said. "I believe he has a broken leg."

ALI SAT IN the back seat holding Bob as Jax drove toward Winchester. He had called Holloway, and he'd made arrangements. Burt Johnston was more than happy to meet them at his veterinary clinic in Winchester.

"Did you get lost or spooked, boy?" Ali rubbed his head and wished she could do something for the pain. His nose was warm, and his respiration was quick and shallow. She felt so helpless.

"I'm thinking he got outside and chased some animal that wandered into the yard. He got too close to the edge and slipped over. Broke his leg in the fall."

Ali cringed. Couldn't bear to picture him falling.

"Considering the drop, I'm surprised he's not hurt worse."

"Are we almost there?" She had no idea where the clinic was. Wherever it was, getting there was taking far too long.

"According to my GPS, we're almost there."

Ali stroked the animal and hummed softly to him. It was the strangest thing, but he liked when she hummed to him—like a kid. She smiled. She wondered if Bob was the closest thing to a child she would ever have. How could she have gone her whole life and not known the love of a dog?

"Here we go," Jax said as he slowed for a turn.

Relief rushed through her. "It'll be okay soon, boy."

A man who looked to be around their age met them in the parking lot.

He opened the back door and reached in to stroke Bob. The dog tensed. "Easy now." He looked to Ali and then to Jax. "I'm Tommy Wright, one of Burt's vet techs. We should get this guy inside."

It took some maneuvering, but they finally got him out and into the man's arms. "What's his name?"

"Bob, and I'm Ali—Alice Stewart," she said. "He's four years old and, to my knowledge, in good health. I hope he's not hurt too badly. He fell quite a distance."

Holding the door, Jax said, "About eight feet."

When Tommy had gone through the door, Ali followed. Jax closed the door. She heard the click of the automatic lock.

"What do we have here?" A tall, older man asked as they entered what looked like an operating room.

Tommy repeated what Ali and Jax had told him.

"I'm Burt, by the way." The older man glanced at her and smiled. "The best vet in these parts, and the county coroner."

A smile spread across her lips despite the worry twisting inside her. Burt Johnston was seventy-five if he was a day. His demeanor was kind and even a bit charming. She was grateful.

"Why don't you two have a seat in the corridor beyond that door and we'll take care of Bob."

As much as it pained her to leave him, Ali did as Burt asked. Jax sat in the hard, plastic chair next to her. When they had sat in silence for a while, her gaze glued to the activities beyond the open door, she pulled her attention to the man beside her.

"Thank you for rescuing him."

"Holloway says he's in the best hands available with Burt. He's been taking care of animals his entire life."

Another smile tugged at her lips. "I wonder how he became the coroner."

Jax chuckled. "I don't know the answer, but I guarantee you it's quite a story."

She sighed. "I miss this."

He turned to her. She didn't have to look—she felt the heat of his stare.

"Sitting in a cold corridor with me?"

She smiled again in spite of herself. "No. I mean, the small-town way of life. Everyone knows everyone else. Neighbors help each other out. I didn't realize until now how much I missed that sense of family."

"I know what you mean," he said.

She turned to him, surprised. "I thought you were all about the city."

Wasn't his desire to go to Seattle in part about being part of a thriving city atmosphere?

"Seattle is a nice city. Going there was about being close to my family. As you recall, they live only an hour outside Seattle, in a small town very much like Winchester."

"Right." She wanted to throw in that she'd forgotten, but that would be a lie. She remembered everything about his family.

"Why did you move to Nashville?"

She shouldn't be asking personal questions since she certainly didn't want to answer any of his, but she had to know. He'd wanted to get back to Seattle so badly ten years ago. Why the sudden change of heart?

He shrugged. "It was a career move. I won't be here long. Maybe another year at the most. If all goes well, I'll end up back in the Seattle area with the experience I need for a supervisory position. If it works out, I'll be there for the rest of my career."

"Oh." It was the only thing she could think to say. He had a long-range plan.

"What about you?"

"I just want to get through Thursday, and then I'll go from there."

They both fell silent, staring straight ahead. The urge to ask him if there was someone in Nashville or back home—someone special—prodded her.

No. She wouldn't ask.

"You can start over. Put all this behind you." He looked at her but she couldn't meet his gaze. "You never have to look back, Ali."

Burt started toward the door, and she stood. Anything to move on from the moment.

"Is he going to be okay?"

Burt nodded. "He surely is. We'll need to keep him overnight. Make sure nothing else crops up considering he took quite the tumble. You can pick him up tomorrow afternoon."

Ali wasn't sure what to say to that. Tomorrow afternoon she would be in Atlanta, readying for trial.

"We'll actually be out of town for the next couple of days," Jax explained. "Can he stay until we're back?"

She darted a glance at Jax. He was awfully confident she would be coming back. Her stomach suddenly rolled, and she fought the urge to heave.

Nerves, she reminded herself. She would get through this.

"Certainly. We'll take very good care of him."

The last part he directed to Ali. "Would you like to say goodbye? He's sedated now so he might be a little woozy."

"Thank you."

Bob didn't raise his head as she came nearer, but his eyes followed her movement. She stroked his head and whispered in his ear.

She would be back for him.

Somehow.

Chapter Ten

It felt strange to be completely alone with Jax.

Bob had been a sort of buffer, at least in Ali's mind.

She sat on the sofa now, staring at the fire. It was late. She should go to bed. Tomorrow was a big day. The day after would be an even bigger one.

But sleep would not be possible. Not just now.

The one question she had been asked today would be the hardest to answer on Thursday.

Why did you stay after you found out what he was?

Shock, disbelief…fear.

She had asked him about the reaction of her co-volunteers. From that moment he had known that the fantasy was over.

I knew the truth—at least a small fraction of that truth.

In today's world of fearless women and total independence, no woman on the jury would understand her simple truth.

When she was in college and then after when she started her career, she had heard friends say that no man would ever rule them. Ali remembered feeling exactly the same way, especially considering how Jax had broken her heart.

But Harrison had been different. He had not been a mere man. He had been a monster. Taught by the mother of all monsters…his father.

Ali had been lucky to escape with her life.

If the jury chose not to believe her story, she could do nothing to change their minds. All that mattered was that they believed her when she stated who had shot and murdered the man to whom she had been married.

Nothing else about the trial mattered. It was not about her redemption or somehow proving she was not a total fool. It was about taking that bastard all the way down.

Jax was suddenly standing over her. She hadn't heard him come into the room.

"You should eat."

How many times had he suggested she eat the past few days? She was not a child. She could decide for herself when to eat.

"If I wanted to eat, I would eat." Her tone was far sharper than she'd intended.

He lowered to the coffee table, settling there so that he sat directly across from her. Too close. She drew back into the sofa cushion.

"Thursday I'll be in that courtroom with you. If

there is anything you want to discuss with me now, it might make that day easier."

She stared at him then. Why did he care? "I'll be answering the questions in front of all sorts of strangers. Why would I feel any differently about you?"

Her words hit their mark. He flinched.

"Because I want to hear them from you before all those strangers."

She was tired. Tired of all the pomp and circumstance of preparing for this trial. Tired of being protected. Tired of being alone.

When this was over, no one who had been involved with this case would care what happened to her. She would be left to fend for herself. Anger ignited in her chest. She wasn't a person to those people who wanted so desperately to destroy the Armone family. She was evidence. Nothing more.

She looked directly into his dark eyes now. Eyes she had gazed into and gotten lost in all those years ago. "You want to hear all the dirty details of how he kept me in line? What prevented me from running away and going to the authorities sooner?"

He didn't answer, just sat there staring at her with such concern and regret. Yes, regret. She wanted to laugh out loud. *He* regretted what she had gone through. He most likely had no idea exactly what that was. But he understood it was bad.

"All right. I'll tell you why I stayed until the day I watched his father put a bullet in his head."

He swallowed hard, then visibly braced himself.

In that clarifying moment, she understood without doubt that he already knew something. Part of her ugly story, at least.

Maybe he would even enjoy hearing her say the words. Only one way to find out. "At first he assigned a full-time bodyguard to me. I wasn't allowed to go into a bathroom without him. I wasn't allowed to walk around the gated and guarded property without my personal guard at my side. At night one ankle was shackled to the bed."

She shrugged. "Maybe he worried that I would kill him in his sleep and try to run. This way, if I did shove a knife into his chest or use a hammer to bash in his head, I was stuck with his dead body."

She had considered both those methods for freeing herself. She closed her eyes for a moment. Not once in her life had she ever considering harming another human being until then. Thank God her parents were long gone. They would have been so ashamed of her.

"How long did this go on?"

His voice was too soft. She didn't want his pity. She looked away from him. "We had been married a year and a half when one of the other volunteers at the center asked me if I was his wife. One by one, over the next couple of weeks, they all started to shun me. Eventually I asked him if there was something he failed to tell me before we married. Things went downhill from there."

Jax shook his head. "How did you survive?"

She laughed. "I can tell you I wished for death many times, but it didn't come." Her mind went back to those darkest days. "Once I even asked my guard to kill me." She closed her eyes and thought of the look on Tate's face. He had laughed and told her she was trying to get him killed.

And she *had* gotten him killed.

The burden sat heavily on her shoulders...on her heart.

"Harrison could have killed me." Another shrug. "At first I didn't understand why he didn't. I slowly realized that he didn't want me dead. He wanted to punish me for taking away his fantasy. With me he could pretend he wasn't who he really was. He could be the wealthy businessman whose wife spent her time helping those less fortunate. The man whose wife looked at him with such adoration and respect. But I took that away from him. I suppose in part he wanted to keep up the facade. I helped him represent a different life than the one he actually lived."

"He would have had to admit that he'd made a mistake," Jax suggested.

She looked straight at him again. "Men don't like to admit when they've made a mistake. I have the scars to prove it."

He lowered his head, staring at the floor before she could get a glimpse of his reaction to that revelation.

Did he think she'd been held prisoner for more than three years and escaped unscathed? How nice that would have been.

She didn't want to do this anymore. Her emotions were churning, and she just wanted to escape the memories...the feelings. When she would have stood and announced as much, his words stopped her.

"I made a mistake."

He lifted his gaze to hers, and for several beats she couldn't move. She could only stare at him, searching his eyes for the sincerity in his words.

Then the realization that it didn't matter slammed into her chest, forcing the air out of her lungs. She launched to her feet. "Well, this has been..." There was no way to describe how this felt. "Anyway, I'm calling it a night."

He stood, putting himself toe to toe with her. "I made a mistake."

She didn't want to look at him. Didn't want to see what he might show her. But her body had a mind of its own apparently. Her eyes met his. "You said that already."

"I'd barely settled in out in Seattle when I realized that. We were so young. I figured we had time. So I kept an eye on you."

His words took her aback. "What do you mean, you kept an eye on me?"

"I checked on you. I had friends in Glynco. I had them make sure you were doing okay. That's how I knew when your father got sick."

What was he saying? This made no sense. She shook her head. "Why didn't you simply call me?"

"Pride? Stupidity? Take your pick."

This was a pointless waste of time and emotion. "I really—"

"I almost came back. I knew how hard things were for you."

A realization barreled into her. "It was you."

Surprise flared in his eyes then he blinked it away. "I don't—"

"That private nurse who came to help with my dad because we couldn't afford to hire help…that was you."

The nurse had said a private donor paid her salary. She would never say who. Ali had assumed it was some of her father's friends who had gotten together and pooled their resources. God knew they had brought food every day. But she should have realized none of them could afford such a luxury any more than she could.

"My family pitched in, too," he confessed. "We wanted to help."

Ali held up her hands. This was too much. "I genuinely appreciate what you and your family did. I can't tell you how comforting it was to have a nurse to help."

Tears burned her eyes, but she couldn't let him see. Her chest felt so full she would hardly manage a breath.

"When you went back to college, I was really happy for you. I knew how much that meant to you. I thought maybe when you finished I'd show up at your graduation and give you a hug to congratulate or something."

"I'm sorry, I really don't understand why you just didn't call." This made no sense.

"I thought there was time. I didn't want to interfere with you finishing college. I was working hard to establish my career. Move up the ranks."

If he was watching her, why on earth hadn't he stopped her from marrying the bastard?

Before she could demand an answer to that question, he said, "I was sent on an extended undercover assignment, and while I was off the grid, you moved to Atlanta and got married."

So he did know. "You knew I had married into that family and you didn't warn me?"

This time she damaged him. Her demand shook him. His face told the story.

"I couldn't see how you didn't know what he was. I thought you'd decided you wanted what he had to offer regardless of who and what he was."

How could he have thought such a thing? "Then you didn't really know me at all."

He stopped her when she would have moved away from him. His hands seemed to burn her skin through the sweater she wore. "I was wrong." He shook his head. "My ego was bruised. I thought that if you married someone else, you couldn't possibly have cared about me the same way I did about you. I was jealous. Shocked. Torn up. I never checked on you again."

Whether he knew her as well as he should have, she did know him. He meant what he said. She had hurt him by marrying Harrison. But how could she have known Jax still cared or that Harrison was a monster?

"For that," he said, his fingers tightening around her arms as if he feared she would run away, "I am truly sorry. It's my fault this happened to you. Instead of turning my back, I should have come to you and told you the truth. We could have worked things out. But I couldn't see past my bruised ego."

She searched his eyes, felt the weight of his pain for her. "I wished a thousand times that you would show up and rescue me." She laughed, tears slipping down her cheeks no matter how hard she tried to hold them back. "I thought of you so often. I think those little fantasies of you showing up to carry me away from the nightmare are what kept me from giving up." Ali sucked in a sharp breath. "But you never came."

"I'm here now, and I will keep you safe. I can't change the mistakes of the past, but I can make sure they don't happen again. I will not let Armone touch you."

All those months that had run into years, she had longed to hear this man say those words. But now that was the part of all this that terrified her the most. She fully understood how ruthless Armone was. He wouldn't hesitate to have Jax murdered. If he had the slightest idea Ali had feelings for Jax, he would relish the act of taking his life.

She had realized when she arrived in Nashville this morning that she had only one opportunity to do what she had to do. She'd already tried with Holloway, and it hadn't worked out. But it was done now.

"I was thankful you weren't in the room for most of the meeting this morning."

Tension riffled through him, tightening his hold on her even more. "Why is that?"

"I spoke to AUSA Knowles. I told him I didn't want you in Atlanta. He agreed that having you there would be a mistake. So once the plane lands in Atlanta, you'll get on a flight back to Nashville. You won't be leaving the airport. Another marshal will take over from there."

Anger flashed in his eyes. "I see what you're doing. You think you need to protect me. You're wrong." He pulled her closer—too close. "I can take care of myself. I don't need you protecting me."

She stared at his lips as he spoke. No matter that she hated herself for doing it, she couldn't help herself.

"I will call Knowles and straighten this out. There is no way I will let you out of my sight. If they try and stop me, they'll have a fight on their hands."

Worry that she'd made yet another mistake twisted inside her. "You can't do that."

"Oh yes, I can. This time I'm making sure nothing

happens to you. I took my eyes off you once. That won't happen again."

More tears spilled down her cheeks, and she wanted to scream at herself for falling apart.

Then he kissed her. Slow and deep and sweet. The way he had kissed her hundreds of times before. She remembered his taste, every nuance of the way he kissed. And her heart ached with longing.

She could not do this. If she let herself fall this time and he left again, she wouldn't survive it. She wasn't strong enough.

She pressed her palms to his chest, for one single moment savored the feel of him, and then she pushed him away. "We can't do this."

"Yes—" he pressed his forehead to hers "—we can."

She pulled free of his hold, her knees bumping the sofa. "*I* can't."

Moving as quickly as she dared with tears clouding her vision, she hurried up the stairs. A long hot bath would help. Then she was going to go to bed and attempt to sleep.

Tomorrow was the beginning of the end.

ALI HAD NEVER been so grateful for a tub. Usually she preferred showers, but after this day she needed a long, hot soak. Strangely enough, she'd found some bubble bath under the sink, and all the necessities were available. Towels. Soap. Shampoo. She suspected the kind sheriff had ensured those items were on hand. He'd stocked the fridge and a few items in the pantry, too.

Winchester and the surrounding communities were growing on her. So many of the people she had met were so nice.

Once the tub was full enough and bubbles frothed up to the rim, she peeled off her clothes and slid into the welcoming heat. Her entire body sighed. She laid her head back, closed her eyes and did something not so smart by allowing that kiss to fill her senses. The way he'd tasted—pure Jax. In a hundred years, she wouldn't have forgotten his taste. His strong arms around her had made her feel completely safe and far too needy.

"Don't make another mistake," she murmured. Whether the words were an order or a plea for strength, she wasn't sure she could hold back if he came near her again.

She had dreamed of kissing him, making love with him a thousand times—perhaps more—over the past decade. Even when her monster of a husband had held her in his arms, she had found it necessary to push aside the memories of Jax. He had been such a part of her...so deeply entrenched in her soul.

She sighed. Let go of the last of the tension and sank more deeply into the sweet-smelling bubbles. Her muscles slowly grew completely pliable. She felt as if she could melt into the hot water and just slip away.

Except tomorrow was coming, and there was no way to change what she had to do.

If Jax stood between her and a bullet—

She squeezed her eyes shut and blocked the images.

If something happened to him because of her—she couldn't live with that. There had to be a way to prevent him from going to that courthouse with her. She slid beneath the water, allowed it to cover her completely. She lay there for a half a minute, listening to the heavy sounds of the beating of her heart. Then she sat up, pushed her hair back from her face, pulled her knees to her chest and pressed her cheek to them.

She closed her eyes again and allowed memories of their time together to fill her. Maybe it was selfish, but she needed so badly to feel alive again, even if only for this one moment. Her body shivered with an abrupt rush of need. She should have responded more deeply to his kiss. Lost herself in his touch.

Who knew what tomorrow would bring?

What did it matter who did what ten years ago? He had been looking after her those first few years. Maybe if she hadn't married that bastard, things would have been different. Jax would have come back for her.

Why hadn't she swallowed her pride and gone after him once her father passed away? She could have looked him up, said hello and…

But she had been too hurt by his leaving.

Lonely and alone.

A dangerous recipe, which led to utter disaster.

"Ali." He knocked softly at the door. "Can I come in?"

She hugged her arms around her knees more tightly. Did she dare? When he looked at her body, he wouldn't see the smooth flawless skin from ten years ago. There were scars. Small and not so deep, but so many of them.

Could she bear the pity on his face when he saw them?

"I don't want to talk anymore." She pressed her forehead to her knees. Squeezed her eyes shut.

If he came in and saw all of her, there would be more questions.

Could she bear to tell him all the things that bastard had done to her? How he had nearly broken her? Actually, he had broken her, and somehow after witnessing his life ending, she had pulled herself together enough to run.

She should have trusted Jax all those years ago. Should have followed him to Seattle. Coming home to take care of her father wouldn't have been a problem. Jax would have understood. Still, she wouldn't trade those last months with her father for anything. As certain as she was of that, she was also certain her father would not have wanted her to suffer the way she had the past few years.

Before his death he had asked her twice what happened to the nice young man who was training to be a marshal. She never told him that she had given him up to stay close to home.

All of that was behind her now. It was very possible that in another twenty-four hours she would be dead. Why deny herself this time with Jax? Whether she lived or died, he would move on to his next assignment and it wouldn't be her.

He would be gone.

"Come in." The words were out of her mouth before she could stop them. Her mind still resisted, but her heart and the rest of her no longer wanted to refrain.

The door creaked open, and he walked inside. She was thankful for the deep bubbles. Maybe he wouldn't see.

He knelt next to the tub, his forearms resting on the edge. "I'm sorry."

She frowned, searched his dark eyes. "Sorry for what?"

"I should have manned up and come after you when your father was sick. I could have brought both of you to Seattle. I was a fool, and you paid a terrible price."

"I appreciate you saying so, but it wasn't your fault. You did what was right for you. Far too often we don't do that, and it's usually a mistake. When you left, I wanted to go. Desperately. I should have. I should have gone to my father and told him we were moving. I shouldn't have used him as an excuse. I should have done what was right for me. His health was already deteriorating. Looking back, I believe there was a good possibility he would have agreed."

"Hindsight," he said, his lips smiling just a little, "is twenty-twenty. What you know now and what you knew then are two different things. You did the right thing." He shrugged. "Maybe we both did, but there were consequences, and I am truly sorry you suffered the brunt of them."

Tears slipped past her restraint. "Thank you."

He reached for the shampoo. "Let me help you out with this bath. You deserve a little pampering."

He washed her hair, slowly, using his fingers to massage her scalp until she felt ready to moan. She ducked under the water and rinsed the shampoo away. When she surfaced again he washed her back, touching each tiny scar. She shivered. Hated for him to see. Then he leaned forward and kissed her skin, over and over.

As he kissed his way up her neck, he shed his shirt. She reached out and unfastened his jeans. When he'd toed off his shoes and peeled off his jeans and socks, the boxers went next.

And then he was in the water with her.

The feel of his body against hers cleared all the hurt and worry from her mind. She could only feel his skin sliding against her own. His hard body pressing all the soft, needy places of hers.

The sense of belonging…of being home filled her. Whatever else happened, *this* was right in every way.

When his mouth covered hers, she stopped thinking at all.

Chapter Eleven

One day until trial

Wednesday, February 5

Ali stared at herself in the mirror over the bathroom sink. Today they would drive to Huntsville, Alabama. It was less than an hour away. There was an airport there. She would be on the noon flight to Atlanta. Yesterday it had been decided that a commercial flight would be safer than driving. A more controlled situation, AUSA Knowles had said.

Jax hadn't agreed, but he had been overruled. Last night he hadn't mentioned his concerns, and she hadn't asked.

She had needed to escape.

Her eyes closed as her mind immediately replayed their lovemaking. Even though she had loved Harrison in the beginning, her feelings for him had been different than her feelings for Jax. Their intimacy had been completely different. She had no other experience to which to compare, but being with Jax was in a whole other league. There was a depth to their connection that had been missing with Harrison. The absolute certainty that they were meant for each other had never been present in her marriage.

Whatever happened tomorrow, she would cherish last night. This time she understood things were different. They were both mature adults and had their own lives to get back to. Not that she had much of a life anymore. She would be busy—assuming she survived beyond the trial—building a new life. After last night, it was easy to picture that life with Jax wherever his career took him.

But she wasn't foolish enough to believe that one night of lovemaking and truckloads of guilt had resurrected what he had once felt for her.

They were different people now.

She studied her reflection again. The glimpse of fear in her blue eyes tied a knot in her belly. She was no longer that naive young woman. Of course she was a little afraid. But that fear would not stop her from going into that courtroom and telling the truth.

Nine months she had waited to tell the judge and jury the sort of monster Harrison Armone Sr. was. She had been fully apprised of her rights. Instructions on how to proceed with her testimony had been drilled into her head. She had been questioned and cross-examined in an attempt to confuse and frighten her, since this was what would happen in the courtroom.

She was ready.

A dark suit—skirt and jacket—as well as conservative flats had been provided for her to wear. She was to arrange her hair in a twist or bun so that she looked more reserved. No makeup or jewelry. She never wore makeup, anyway. Wore very little jewelry except when her husband had insisted.

Ali turned away from the mirror and left the bathroom. She couldn't hide any longer. She had still been asleep when Jax got up this morning. When she had awakened, she had smelled the delicious scent of coffee brewing. She'd showered and dressed, taking her time.

It wasn't as if they hadn't made love before, she reminded herself as she descended the stairs. But this was different. She hadn't seen him in a decade. He had seen her more recently. She'd been stunned at the idea that he had looked in on her and that he and his family were the ones to help with the private nurse. She needed to write a letter to his mother. Such a dear, sweet lady. How nice it would have been to have her for a mother-in-law. Ali imagined she was an amazing grandmother.

The yearning for children wrapped around her heart and tightened. Ali stopped at the bottom of the stairs and marveled at the sudden reawakening. It had been so long since she dared wish for anything normal. But, she realized, she wanted a family. A real husband and at least two children.

Had making love with Jax roused those long-forgotten hopes and dreams?

As if the idea had summoned him, he was suddenly at the kitchen doorway, smiling. "Good morning."

She had been certain this morning would be awkward. That she would be embarrassed. But she wasn't, at all. Instead, she melted instantly. He was the most beautiful man she had ever met. "Good morning. You were up early."

As she walked toward him, her heart started to pound and her pulse raced. She would love nothing better than to make love with him again, right now. When he'd left the bed this morning, his absence had pulled her from the most magnificent sleep she had experienced in years.

"I checked the perimeter. Made coffee and whipped up a little breakfast."

A smile pulled at her lips, and her stomach reacted to the delicious smells coming from the kitchen. Looking at him had blocked all other stimuli, but his words drew her senses beyond him.

"Smells wonderful."

"Pancakes," he said, stepping aside so that she could walk into the kitchen. "Tanner is a good shopper. He didn't forget the syrup."

As good as the pancakes smelled, Ali walked straight to the coffeemaker. She filled a mug and took a sip, relishing the taste and the heat.

Jax touched her arm and she turned to face him. "Come sit with me."

She allowed him to usher her to the table. They

took their seats, and she smiled at the not quite round pancakes.

"They're a little misshapen, but they taste good." He added a couple more to his plate and drizzled syrup over them.

Ali did the same. "Thank you. This is very nice."

She drizzled the syrup and then took a bite. He was right, the pancakes were really good. "Yum," she said and watched his smile broaden to a grin.

"I've learned a few things living alone all these years."

She didn't say as much, but Ali wished she had been with him all these years. They would likely have children by now. A sigh whispered out of her, and she quickly poked another bite of pancakes into her mouth.

He sipped his coffee then set the mug aside. "I'm certain now that my mother was correct."

Ali cradled her mug of coffee, warming her hands. It was cold this morning. The fire was roaring but still, it was chilly. Or maybe it was just nerves.

"I told you about Seth, my little brother."

The memory tugged at her heart. "You did. Yes. It was a such a tragedy. I'm certain it devastated your entire family."

He nodded, stared at his now empty plate. "My parents have told me hundreds of times that it wasn't my fault, but I couldn't change how I felt."

"Your parents were right. You were a child yourself. You did everything you could. More, actually."

Ali remembered the story vividly. The family had been at their lake house. Jax and Seth had gone fishing on the pier. He had told his little brother repeatedly to stay away from the edge, but he hadn't listened.

When he fell in, Jax tried to save him. The autopsy confirmed that Seth had hit his head on the way down, so he'd been unconscious when he hit the water. Rather than struggling to reach the surface, he had sunk like a rock to the very bottom of the murky depths. Jax almost drowned going down over and over trying to find him.

By the time he did, it was too late.

His hands were flat on the table on either side of his plate, his gaze focused there as if the answer he needed would come to him. "I should have watched him closer. Made him sit down."

"Even the coroner said that it would have been sheer luck to have found him in time. The water was too dark around the bottom." She hated to see him carry that burden. He'd only spoken of that day once in all the time they were together. Yet it was more than apparent that it was with him every day, particularly back then.

He nodded, finally lifted his gaze and met hers. "My mother swears this is why I'm not in a long-term relationship. She says I don't trust myself to take care of a family." He grunted. "She believes the reason I became a marshal was to prove to myself that I could save lives. But nothing I do is ever enough, according to her." He searched Ali's eyes for a moment before saying the rest. "She says it's the reason I let you get away."

Ali's breath stalled in her throat. She, too, had wondered if that long-ago loss had kept him from wanting to fully commit, but she had been too young to trust her own instincts. It was easier to believe that he just hadn't loved her as much as she loved him.

"Your mother was right, Jax. It wasn't your fault, and maybe you have been afraid to commit fully. If you recognize that now, you can choose differently moving forward." This conversation was too much. She couldn't do this. She stood, her chair scooting back. "Thank you for breakfast. It was very nice."

She took her plate and fork to the sink. Since he had cooked, she could certainly do the cleanup. That was the way it was done, wasn't it?

He moved to her side, placing his plate and fork in the sink on top of hers.

She grabbed a paper towel from the roll and readied to wash their dishes. She couldn't look at him. That awkwardness she had feared this morning was now thick between them—at least from her perspective. She couldn't get enough air into her lungs. Her skin was on fire just being near him.

"I was wrong, Ali. I shouldn't have left without you. I've always believed a person made his own fate happen. Whether this moment was fate or not, we have an opportunity here. The potential for a do-over. And we can do it right this time."

Her hands stilled, suds dripping from her skin. How long had she dreamed of hearing those words? How often during those first years after he left had she heard the doorbell or the phone and rushed to answer, hoping it would be him?

But she had been disappointed every time. Then she had run headlong into that horrible mistake of a marriage. From that moment she had known there was never any hope that she would see Jax again. Having a life with him was never, ever going to happen. Her dream had shattered, and she had clung to a new one that turned out to be a living nightmare.

She turned to the man standing so close beside her. He was right. They did have an opportunity here, but she was terrified it wasn't what it seemed. "It's possible," she said, the words hardly able to squeeze out around the lump in her throat, "that what you're feeling right now is nothing more than guilt."

He started to argue with her, but she stopped him. "You felt guilty, which is why you helped when my father passed away." She didn't want to believe her own words—she wanted to believe that he had done it because he cared, but she couldn't take that risk. "When you learned I had married into the Armone family, you were angry. You despised me, I imagined."

"No." He shook his head. "I—"

She held up her hand, stop-sign fashion. "Don't lie to yourself now, Jax. It's time we both faced the truth about our lives. We made mistakes, yes. You made far better choices than me. I made terrible mistakes, and I paid—" she drew in a sharp breath "—for those mistakes."

The pain on his face told her she'd read him right. He was only human.

"Whatever you think," he said, "you're wrong. *This* isn't about guilt."

When she would have argued, he touched his fingers to her lips. "Whether you've ever fully trusted me or not," he said, "trust me now. I know what I feel. I know what I want."

She closed her eyes to block the hope in his. This was far too important to take the plunge without being absolutely certain. Deep breath. She opened her eyes and met his, that desperate hope in his squeezing her heart.

"I trust you completely, Jax." She hated herself as that hope evolved into happiness. "But I don't want a relationship with you based on anything other than the real thing. True love and nothing else."

His hands dived into her hair and clasped her face. "I love you, Ali. If I ever doubted that, I was wrong."

Her damp hands rested against his chest to slow things down. Her heart felt ready to burst. "I want that to be true. So very, very much. But we're in a high-pressure place right now. Fear and desperation make people do things they normally wouldn't do."

He stroked her cheek with his thumb. "I won't change my mind tomorrow or the day after or the day after that."

"Let's make a deal, then." It was so incredibly difficult to think clearly with him touching her, looking at her this way. But she had to be strong, had to think clearly. This was far too important. "When this is over, if you still feel the same way, we'll give us a new go."

He turned her face up so he could gaze deeply into her eyes. "Count on it."

Then he kissed her, and her fingers fisted in his shirt with longing.

Before the moment got completely out of control, she drew her lips from his. Pressed her forehead to his chin.

If she lived through this day and the next, she was going to spend the entire weekend making love with this man somewhere far away from here.

JAX WATCHED ALI come down the stairs with the garment carrier that held her trial clothes. Over her shoulder she'd slung the backpack that held the rest of her things.

"Let me help you with those."

When she reached the bottom step, he took the two bags. "I'll put these in the car with mine."

"Thanks."

Taking his eyes from her was not easy, but he managed. They'd made a deal, and for now he had to focus on keeping her safe. He couldn't allow anything to distract him.

As he exited the house, he scanned the perimeter.

Once he'd tucked the bags into the cargo area, he locked the SUV and did a walk around. It was damn cold, but otherwise all was as it should be.

Back inside, he heard Ali talking in the kitchen. He locked the door and moved in that direction.

"I know," she said.

She was using the small cell phone Holloway had given her.

"It's a lot to ask," she sighed, "but I'd feel better if I knew Bob was going to be okay. If you can't take him, Marshal Holloway, I understand."

She was making arrangements for the dog in case she didn't make it. Jax closed his eyes and steadied himself. All these emotions were tricky. Keeping his head screwed on straight was the most important part of what he had to do right now.

"Thank you. I really appreciate it." Pause. "Yes, I checked with Dr. Johnston, and he said Bob is doing great." Another pause. "I will. Thank you for everything, Marshal. You made the past six months bearable."

She ended the call and tucked the phone into her hip pocket.

"You'll be taking care of Bob yourself," he said.

She turned, surprised that he was standing so close. She nodded. "Hope so."

He was the one drawing in an extra-deep breath now. "It's time to go."

"Okay."

They walked through the house, made sure everything was turned off. Jax flipped the breaker for the hot water heater to the off position, and then he locked the door behind them.

Ali squared her shoulders and walked to his SUV. He opened her door, waited for her to buckle up and then closed it. Their eyes met for a moment, and the fear in hers tore him apart inside.

He loaded up, turned the SUV around and headed down that narrow road.

Just as they crossed the stream, his cell vibrated on the console. He picked it up. *Holloway.*

"What's up?"

He supposed his friend just wanted to ensure they were ready and on the road.

"There's been a change of plans."

Holloway's voice sounded as surprised and frustrated as Jax suddenly felt. "What kind of change?"

He glanced at Ali. She stared back at him with mounting uncertainty.

"AUSA Knowles is concerned about the commercial flight now."

"Fine," Jax said before he could continue. "I prefer driving." He would be more in control of the situation that way.

"He still won't agree to highway transport. He wants her on a plane."

What the hell? "So where are we going?"

"There's a private plane waiting at the Winchester Municipal Airport. Special Agent Wesley McEntire is waiting with the pilot."

Last-minute changes always made Jax nervous. But it happened. There were people whose job it was to assess transport options all the way down to the wire.

"Okay. Give me the directions." He listened as Holloway listed off the streets and turns he would need to make to reach the small local airport. "Thanks. I'll confirm when we're in the air."

"Good luck, Stevens. Take good care of her."

"If it's the last thing I do," he assured him.

He dropped his cell back on the console.

"I take it we're not going to the airport in Huntsville."

The slight hitch in her breathing as she spoke twisted his gut. "They've decided we're taking a private plane from the airport here in Winchester."

"Okay."

She stared forward. He did the same.

"Is it normal to have last-minute changes on a day like today?"

She didn't glance his way, and her words sounded stilted. He hated that she was afraid. Wished he could assure her, but every instinct he possessed warned that this was wrong somehow. Risky.

He glanced in the rearview mirror. No one behind them. He slowed and pulled to the side of the road.

She stared at him, worry clouding her face. "What's wrong?"

He hesitated, but then he said what he felt. "We don't have to do this."

"I don't understand."

"We can drive away. Go someplace where that bastard will never find you."

He sounded as if he'd gone over the edge. He recognized this. But the urge to take her out of this scenario and someplace else was overwhelming.

"No." She shook her head. "Your career would be over, and that monster would walk away scot-free. I have to do this, Jax. There is no other choice."

She was right. He didn't know what he'd been thinking.

Before he could apologize, she leaned across the console and kissed him. "Thank you for caring so much."

He forced a smile. "Let's do this, then."

Every nerve ending in his body was humming with a warning.

His instincts had only failed him once, and that had been ten years ago—when he walked away from this woman.

Chapter Twelve

The airport was smaller than she had expected.

A man in a dark suit identified himself as FBI, producing his credentials. Ali watched from the passenger seat of Jax's SUV as he spoke with the agent. He had told her to stay in the vehicle until he checked things out.

Her nerves were vibrating, making her restless. She wanted to get on that plane, get to Atlanta and finish this. Most of all she wanted Jax to come through this unharmed, and for the first time since all this began, she desperately wanted to survive. For months she had hoped to survive, but if she didn't—so be it. She would do this no matter how the circumstances ended for her. But now there was something to look forward to.

Jax wanted to try again.

He still cared about her.

Her pulse started to pound with the thought. She pushed away the tiny doubts that attempted to sprout. He had no reason to mislead her. It wasn't like he was attempting to persuade her to testify. That was a given. He had absolutely nothing to gain by suggesting that they needed to pursue their feelings.

This was real.

Jax returned to the SUV and opened her door. "They're ready."

She was ready, too.

Ready to put the past behind her once and for all.

He stepped to the back of the SUV and grabbed their bags from the cargo area. Ali climbed out and walked across the tarmac with him. They climbed the stairs and stepped into the small jet. Inside there were six leather seats. Jax guided her to the middle row and gestured for her to have a seat.

The jet was small but well equipped. This one was not nearly as large but similar to the one the Armone family owned. Sleek and luxurious from the lighting to the carpet. The seats were heavenly.

The hydraulic sound of the door closing drew their attention forward. Beyond the small partition, the pilot was adjusting controls and speaking into his headset.

Jax moved toward him. "What about the agent?"

The pilot glanced back at him. "My orders are to transport only the two of you." His attention shifted forward once more. "You and the other passenger need to prepare for takeoff. We have a tight schedule. If we don't land on time, they'll call out the cavalry."

Ali's nerves were jumping now. Jax was right—this didn't feel right. The fear and paranoia could be the root of her sudden uneasiness, but she worried that it was more.

When Jax had settled into the seat next to her, he pulled out his cell.

The plane started to roll forward.

Ali focused on breathing. This would not be a good time for a panic attack. Flying had never bothered her before, but today was different.

Jax dropped his cell back into his jacket pocket. "There's no service."

His tension made her all the more anxious.

To hold herself together, she focused on the mundane. She fastened her safety belt. Jax did the same.

"How long does this flight take?" She hugged her arms around herself. Cold had seeped into every part of her.

"Forty minutes, maybe. Less than an hour for sure."

Less than an hour. Good. "A car will pick us up and take us to the hotel?"

"Holloway said that had all been arranged by a Marshal Steadman from the Atlanta office."

"I remember him," she said, thinking back to the first big teleconference she'd participated in after arriving in Kentucky. She didn't remember him commenting during the meeting, but he had been at the table.

"Try to relax," he suggested. "This may be your last opportunity for any semblance of calm. There will likely be meetings this afternoon and final prep for tomorrow."

"I'll try, but no guarantees."

He smiled, and she relaxed the tiniest bit, allowing her arms to settle onto the armrests rather than hugging so tightly around her. His hand settled over hers, fingers lacing. The sensation of being protected slipped over her.

She almost drifted off. She really did, but she couldn't totally relax. Her mind kept going over all that had happened yesterday and last night—Bob's injury, making love with Jax…talk of the future. Excitement shimmered just beneath the worries about tomorrow. She allowed her mind to wander. She would be facing Harrison's father in the courtroom tomorrow. He would be sitting at the defendant's table. She would be in the witness box describing all the heinous details of his life and work.

His evil eyes would stare at her, hoping to intimidate her. She was well aware of the depraved things he did to those who angered or betrayed him. But she had made up her mind that fear was not going to stop her. She would see him go down for all the terrible things he had done.

Her eyes drifted shut, and she almost dozed off. The sound of the pilot's voice stirred her from that place between awake and asleep.

"Marshal Stevens?"

Jax unfastened his safety belt and walked to the front of the aircraft.

Ali leaned forward to hear the exchange. Her heart had started that frantic pounding again.

"We're being diverted," the pilot said.

"On whose order?" Jax asked.

"Marshal Steadman. There's been a security breach with DeKalb-Peachtree. They're diverting us to an airstrip about thirty-nine miles south of Atlanta. We'll prepare for landing in another ten minutes."

"All right."

As he moved back toward his seat, the hard set of his jaw as well as the thin line of his lips told Ali that something beyond another change in the itinerary was wrong. He was not happy about this second change in plans. Her stomach twisted into knots. She wasn't opposed to change—what worried her was his reaction to the changes. Jax had done this for a decade. His instincts were likely well honed. If he was worried, she certainly should be.

"How worried should I be?"

She saw no reason to beat around the bush. The next twenty-four hours were going to determine whether she had a future at all. The possibility that any future she might have could potentially include Jax had her even more determined to survive beyond tomorrow.

"We should be on alert," he said. "Anytime there are security breaches and changes are necessary, the risk factor is elevated."

Ali stared straight ahead. "He doesn't want me to make it to Atlanta. If I don't make it, he walks. I'm sure he would do anything to make that happen."

She gritted her teeth. He could not get away with all he'd done. The fact that he'd murdered his own son wasn't even the worst of his crimes. Particularly since his son had been equally guilty. Ali suppressed a shudder. She had spent most of the past nine months attempting to evict memories of their time together from her mind.

Years would be required to erase him and all that she had seen and experienced.

She turned to Jax. He attempted another call on his cell. No luck. Staying in her seat was becoming more and more difficult by the moment. What if the marshal wasn't waiting for them at the airfield? What if it was Armone? Or some of his goons? They would all be dead within minutes of landing.

His gaze locked with hers. "We'll get through this," he promised.

She had to trust him. To do anything else would make the next minutes and hours unbearable. With that in mind, she mustered up a smile. "We will."

"Descending now," the pilot announced. "We'll be landing soon."

Jax took her hand again and returned her smile. Somehow just seeing his smile boosted her confidence. The plane started to descend, and Ali's pulse thumped harder and harder. Marshal Steadman would be waiting for them. Dozens of people were working on their security. This was, after all, the trial of the century.

Ali stared out the window as they drew closer and closer to the ground. The airfield looked to be nothing more than an airstrip in the middle of nowhere. There were no hangars or other buildings. There was only one small block structure that could possibly be an office.

Jax leaned over her to peer out the window.

There was no car waiting. That grim expression claimed his face once more.

The plane touched down, bounced and then settled back onto the ground again. The wheels bumped along the strip of asphalt. The plane slowed, the inertia forcing them forward in their seats. Her stomach always flip-flopped during landings. She appreciated that the landing was over fairly quickly, if joltingly.

Before stopping completely, the pilot turned the plane around to face the entrance to the airstrip. "Your transportation hasn't arrived yet. Marshal Steadman said you should stay onboard until your car arrives."

For a long minute, they stayed in their seats, just as the pilot had said. Ali stared out the window. The airstrip was so far outside Atlanta that all she could see in any direction were trees. Maybe the isolation was an added layer of security. Armone couldn't possibly have eyes on every airfield and private airstrip in the tri-county area. This was probably a good move.

Jax suddenly stood. He held out his hand. "I think we should wait outside."

She didn't second-guess him or hesitate. She stood and put her hand in his. "I could use some fresh air."

When they started toward the door the pilot repeated, "Marshal Steadman said—"

Jax reached for the weapon in his shoulder holster. "Open the door and lower the stairs."

The pilot, whose name she still didn't know, turned back to the control center and took the necessary action to start the process Jax had requested. The hatch-style door slowly opened, and the staircase lowered to the ground.

Jax moved down the staircase, pulling Ali behind him. When their feet were on the ground and they were clear of the aircraft, Jax pulled her close.

"Something is wrong here." He surveyed the area.

The sound of traffic in the distance suggested they weren't far from an interstate. But here, there was nothing. They could have been back on that mountain outside Winchester. There were no houses in either direction. A two-lane, unlined road with faded asphalt sprawled out in both directions. The problem was she had no idea exactly where they were. Thirty miles south of Atlanta, he had said. Her mind attempted to piece together a map and pinpoint a spot.

"We may have to make a run for it," he said, his gaze steady on the one entrance to the airstrip.

"I can do that." She'd done a good deal of running the last year of her marriage as well as since she'd moved to Winchester. That path she and Bob had traveled every day had been done in a dead run as often as in a leisurely walk.

Ali never wanted to be weak or afraid ever again.

"Pay attention," he said, "and do exactly as I say when I say it."

She nodded, her heart starting to race. "How will we be sure who's coming when the car turns in?"

The windows could be tinted. No one had told them what kind of vehicle Steadman would be driving. Worry gnawed at her.

A black sedan appeared in the distance.

"Looks like our ride," Jax said.

The plane's engine abruptly roared to life. Before the sedan she'd spotted had reached the turn to the airstrip, the plane was rolling toward takeoff at the other end of the airstrip.

"That's our cue," Jax said.

He was right. The pilot wouldn't be taking off before he confirmed that they had been picked up unless he had reason to flee.

He was leaving them here to die.

Jax was suddenly tugging her along behind him.

The plane had lifted off, and the sedan had made its turn. They hit the tree line and plunged into the woods.

Ali had never been more thankful in her life for the cold weather. The chances of stumbling upon a snake were slim to none. Bears would likely still be hibernating. At least she hoped so.

The sound of car doors slamming in the distance warned they wouldn't be running through these woods alone for long.

Chapter Thirteen

Ali ran as fast as she could.

Thank God for the running shoes she wore. And the warm socks and heavy jacket. Though it was warmer here than it had been in Tennessee, it was still cold.

Jax held tight to her hand and plunged through the woods, darting around trees, plowing through underbrush. There was no time to try the quiet route. His goal, she suspected, was to put as much distance between them and the bad guys as possible.

Slow and quiet could come later when they found some sort of cover or had gotten far enough ahead of those giving chase.

Limbs brushed at her legs. Roots snagged at her feet.

Don't fall! Don't fall!

Hang on tight to his hand.

Run.

She clung to his hand with all her strength. His grasp was firm, unrelenting. Her fingers were growing numb, but she ignored it. She had to keep going. Ignore the burn in her lungs. Hang on. Hang on.

A piece of tree bark popped into the air, pinged against her hair.

Then the echoing sound of bullets being fired exploded in her head.

They were shooting at them.

Move faster.

Jax suddenly stopped. She slammed into his back. He pulled her down to a crouch, his finger at his lips in a gesture of quiet.

The thick brush swallowed them.

He pointed to the water that was only steps away. Seemed too wide to be a stream…more like a river. She hadn't even seen it until he pointed at it.

Fear surged through her veins.

They were trapped.

He dropped to his hands and knees and crawled toward the water. She followed. He went in first, crawling until his body floated in the deeper water.

Ice seemed to form around her as she did the same. The water was so cold.

How could they escape like this?

They would surely die of hypothermia first!

He suddenly disappeared.

Her breath caught. Where was he?

His hand tugged her downward.

She inhaled long and deep and slid beneath the surface. The water was murky, but not so dark that she couldn't see the rocky bottom. She wasn't sure how long she could hold her breath.

Suddenly they were in total darkness. She drew back. Needed to surface. He pulled her onward. She needed air. She couldn't stay under any longer.

Suddenly he was pulling her upward. When her face broke the surface of the water, she gasped for air. Her lungs seized with need. Her body quaked from the icy water. He pressed his finger to her lips. She could barely see him. Why was it so dark? Light filtered in, but only a tiny amount.

She forced her brain to think—to analyze their surroundings. The water was up around their waists, not quite to their chests. Sunlight filtered through... limbs and twigs and other natural debris. She understood now. A large tree had fallen into the water and served as a dam-like object, holding fallen limbs and twigs and...wait. She blinked to adjust her eyes. Maybe not all the debris was natural. An old beverage cooler, the disposable kind. What might be a black jacket and other trash.

Distant shouting in the woods snapped her mind back to the danger close by. So damned close.

Jax pulled on her hand. Ali watched as he lowered to his knees, his chin level with the water's surface. She did the same, stretching to keep her nose and eyes above the surface.

The ones chasing them were at the riverbank now. Their voices drifted through the cold, crisp air. She couldn't make out every word, but obviously they were attempting to determine which direction the two of them had taken.

Her body shivered. She struggled to contain the quakes. If she made a sound, she might draw their attention.

Don't move, don't move!

More frantic talking. Judging by their voices, they were extremely disgruntled that they had lost their prey.

She closed her eyes and tried to ignore the odor of the water…of the rotting vegetation and something oddly musky. Where had that odor come from?

Jax squeezed her hand, and her eyes opened. Movement in the water drew her gaze there.

Snake.

Her heart stuttered to a near halt. She held her breath as the urge to flee fired through her veins. That was the musky scent.

Fear clamped like a vise around her chest.

The long brown-and-black body glided along the water's surface.

Ali bit her bottom lip hard to prevent screaming. The sound burgeoned in her throat. Pressed against the back of her teeth.

Had they inadvertently awakened a hibernating snake?

Were there more? Was this their home?

Jax held her hand so tightly she thought her bones might be crushed.

Adrenaline buffeted her chest, roared in her veins. She could barely breathe. Prayed the thing would keep moving.

And it did.

As it glided away, the tension in her body lowered to a more tolerable level. Jax's grasp on her hand loosened a fraction.

She managed a shaky breath without dragging water into her nostrils.

The voices had faded.

Jax waited another minute. Each second ticked off like tiny explosions in Ali's mind. Her body had started to quake. She couldn't stop the reaction to the cold now seeped fully into every muscle and bone in her body.

When they still heard no sound, Jax started to move in the direction away from where they had entered the water.

Keeping their heads down, they progressed through the chest-deep water. A few minutes later, he was pulling her up onto the bank. Her body was numb. She shook uncontrollably.

He burrowed into the underbrush and pulled her into his lap, wrapped his arms around her and held her tight to him.

She closed her eyes and let the shaking overtake her. She couldn't fight it any longer. The air around them was quiet. Not a sound beyond the water moving idly along the banks. Her fingers felt like icicles, her arms and legs like frozen slabs. She had never been so cold in her entire life.

For what felt like hours but was certainly only minutes, they sat there, hugging each other, struggling to absorb each other's body heat—what little there was. He stood, pulling her up with him. She couldn't fathom how he found the strength to do so. She felt weak and shaky.

He pressed his face to hers and whispered, "We're going to move slowly for a while. Staying quiet is our goal."

She nodded her understanding.

Again, he pulled her along, ushering her forward when her body wanted to collapse in on itself.

Their only saving grace after that freezing dip in the water was that it was indeed warmer here than it had been in Tennessee. Still, she was so cold.

But cold was far better than dead.

THEY WALKED FOR what felt like miles. Her shoes still squished with every step, but her clothes were drying in some places. The legs of her jeans were reasonably dry. But the sweatshirt beneath her jacket remained soggy, as did the waist of her jeans.

She was still cold, but not the kind of cold she had been before they began walking. It was doubtful that she would ever truly be completely warm again. Her body was working hard to move quickly across the wooded terrain, which forced her muscles to heat up.

What she would give for a hot cup of coffee.

Jax stopped and listened.

She did the same.

He'd stopped once already to try and use his cell phone, but the water had killed it. They needed dry clothes and a phone, he'd said.

Ali wanted out of these woods. She had no desire to pee behind a tree again.

Jax hadn't said anything else. She understood that keeping quiet was extremely important. If those guys—she had no idea how many there had been—were still after them, they couldn't risk the sound of their voices carrying.

He didn't have to say the words for her to know that he was focused on reaching a phone to call in for more reasons than one.

Someone on his team had sold them out. The marshal, Steadman? The pilot?

When the type of transportation and the place for takeoff had changed, he had sensed something was wrong. She had as well, to a lesser degree. His training had him on the highest level of alertness.

As strong as she considered herself to be, she was depending solely on him to survive this new development.

The stillness in the air, the absence of noise had them moving forward again.

With the sun high in the sky, it had to be nearly noon. She had never appreciated the sun more than this moment. The bare trees allowed the rays to filter down to them. Her hair was dry, thankfully. She imagined it looked a mess, but she could live with a bad hair day. Jax's leather jacket was likely ruined. Like hers, his sneakers still squished now and then.

For the first time since this day began, her stomach reminded her that she hadn't eaten in a long while.

Probably all the physical exertion. She pushed on, keeping pace as best she could with his long strides. Not an easy task. Her legs stung from all the slaps of brush against her jeans, particularly while they were wet.

A faraway honking sound brushed her ears.

Jax stopped. "Did you hear that?"

"Yes."

"We may be getting close to a highway."

He started moving again, pulling her forward through the waist-deep brush and dead grass.

More noise filtered through the trees.

The faintest sound of barking…a dog.

Jax slowed his pace.

Then the reason punched Ali square in the face. *Dogs.*

What if they were being tracked by dogs?

Fear shot through her heart like a bullet.

The barking stopped.

She tightened her grip on his hand. He turned to her. "It wasn't that kind of dog."

Relief flooded her, making her knees weak. She nodded. "Good to know."

They started forward again, moving slower and as quietly as possible.

A wood fence came into view. It seemed to run for acres just beyond the tree line. Beyond the fence were rooftops.

A neighborhood.

More relief gushed through her. After reaching the fence, Jax stretched up and had a look. Ali waited, hoping this was perhaps someplace they could find a phone.

"We'll follow the fence line until we find the end."

She nodded. The going was easier here. For about three feet on this side of the fence line, the underbrush had been cleared. Fatigue was catching up to her now. Her muscles ached, and she was fading fast.

It felt like another mile before they reached a turn in the fence line. A man-made pond stretched out before them. Beyond that was a fenced playground.

Jax reached for her hand, and they started to walk again. Ali felt another shiver; she hoped anyone who looked out their windows would see them as just a couple out for a midday stroll around the pond. Except they likely looked like hell. Bedraggled and grungy. Thankfully it was a school day as well as a workday. If they were lucky, there wouldn't be many people home to see the trespassers.

"Should we just knock on a door?"

Jax was surveying the neighborhood, smiling as if she'd said something funny. "Haven't decided yet."

They walked the block, then made a left onto the next one. The street ended in a cul-de-sac where an empty lot and a home under construction rounded out the street with only one finished house. The finished house looked quite new itself and was for sale. Jax walked to the house under construction and studied it.

"Nice place," Ali said as she too pretended to survey the two-story skeleton of a home.

"It is." He glanced at her. "We're going to walk around the house that's for sale over there and see how difficult it will be to get inside."

"Ready when you are."

They followed the sidewalk to the house with the Realtor's sign in the yard. Jax pulled a detail sheet from the flyer box. From that point, they alternately studied the flyer and explored. They walked up onto the porch and then back down the steps and around the side yard.

"Looks as if someone is living here," Ali noted.

"Sure does. But I'm guessing they aren't home."

"How can you tell?" They were in the backyard now with nothing but trees and a fence that cut between this backyard and the one behind it.

"There were four newspapers in the swing on the porch. All still rolled and in wrappers."

She had noticed the swing but not the newspapers. "But if someone lives here, they probably have a security system."

"Mmm-hmm. But they probably don't have it armed so Realtors don't have to know the code to show the house. Too much of a hassle."

"Are we breaking in?"

"We are."

He walked straight to the rear of the garage, where a walk-through door led from the garage into the backyard. Using a credit card from his sodden wallet, he worked some sort of sleight of hand and opened the door.

"Did you learn that in marshal school?"

He closed the door and locked it. "I learned that in high school, but I'll take the Fifth on the rest of the story." He walked to the door that led into the house. "We won't be so lucky on this one." He tapped the lock. "This one has a dead bolt."

He turned all the way around, checking the garage. There was a sedan parked on one side. A neat row of shelves on the wall beyond it. At the end, near the door they had entered, was a workbench with drawers.

"What we need is a key."

Ali checked under the doormat. Jax felt along the top of the door frame. No key.

He moved to the sedan and checked the wheel wells for one of those magnetic key holders.

"Voilà," he announced.

Ali watched patiently as he unlocked the sedan and searched through it. He climbed out with a key ring loaded with keys.

"Maybe we'll get lucky."

She followed him to the door and watched as he tried key after key. Finally, he grinned. "This is the one."

As he opened the door, she held her breath. If an alarm went off...

But the keypad was not blinking. Jax checked the status. "Unarmed," he said.

He locked the door behind them and tossed the keys on the kitchen counter. There was a phone with a built-in answering machine. Next to it was a list of numbers.

She pointed to one of the numbers. "This one is for a hotel in San Francisco."

Jax picked up the list and turned it over. The homeowner's agenda was written out on that side of the paper. He, she or they had left on Tuesday and wouldn't be back until Sunday.

They were safe for the moment.

"Let's have a walk through before we get comfortable," Jax suggested.

Ali followed him from room to room on the first level, then repeated the same on the second one. He looked for cameras or any other devices that might notify the owner of their presence or record their activities. The master bedroom was the only one that appeared to be in use. The other two bedrooms had very little furniture, and there were no clothes in the closets or drawers.

Back downstairs, they returned to the kitchen and Jax checked the fridge. He grabbed two bottles of water and handed one to her. "Upstairs there was a laundry room. Throw your clothes and shoes in the washer and have a shower. I'll stay down here and make sure no one comes in on us. Once your clothes are washed and dried, you play lookout and I'll do the same."

"Are you going to call Holloway?" He would be worried. "We can trust him." She was certain of that if nothing else.

"I'll call Holloway, and we'll figure out what we do next. You go shower."

He didn't have to twist her arm. She was still cold, and she was so tired she could scarcely remain standing. "Okay."

She forced her weary legs to climb the stairs once more. The master's en suite was gorgeous. Lots of marble and a huge soaker tub. But she needed a shower to rinse all that murky river water off her body. She shuddered as she recalled the snake that had slithered past. But then, they had invaded his habitat.

She walked back to the laundry room and opened the washing machine. She tossed her jacket, shoes and socks inside. Then peeled off her jeans, panties and sweatshirt. Bra, too. She threw the whole lot in the machine and added detergent and fabric softener. With the selection set to a quick wash cycle, she pressed Start and headed back to the shower. She turned on the faucet, set the temperature to hot and rounded up a towel.

For a long minute or two, she stood under the hot spray and allowed the water to rinse and warm her skin. She washed her hair and added some of the conditioner that smelled heavenly. Then she spent a good long while slathering her body with the lavender-and-vanilla body wash.

By the time she stepped out of the shower, she was warm and relaxed and felt relatively human again.

With the towel wrapped around her, she moved her clothes from the washer to the dryer and started the cycle. She padded back to the bathroom and combed her hair. Since she had to wait for the dryer, she might as well blow out her hair.

When she returned to the laundry room, she draped her towel over the hamper. Her panties, bra and socks were dry. With those items on, she walked back to the master bedroom and had a look in the closet. She found a Georgia Bulldogs T-shirt and pulled it on. The hem hit the tops of her thighs. Good enough.

Downstairs, Jax had prepared her a peanut butter sandwich.

"Your turn," she announced. "The rest of my clothes are still drying."

He looked her up and down. "I got no complaints."

She grinned. "Thanks for the sandwich. Did you reach Holloway?"

"I did. I'll tell you all about it after I get this river stench washed off me."

"You will feel like a new man," she promised.

"You keep your eyes and ears open," he called back from the stairs. "We're not in the clear yet."

Her smile faded. This she knew well. There were no guarantees how long they would be safe here.

There were no guarantees about any of this.

Chapter Fourteen

Jax had checked on Ali three times since his five-minute shower. Even five minutes was too long to allow her out of his sight, but one of them had to listen for any potential arrivals. Though the owners were out of town, a Realtor could stop by with a client at any time. For that reason, it was necessary to be vigilant.

He opened the dryer—finally his jeans were dry. He'd hung his jacket up in the garage. He wasn't sure how it would come out.

This was not an ideal situation. Breaking and entering and basically stealing water, electricity and food were not a part of his training. As much as he disliked the idea of doing this, it was necessary for Ali's safety.

Until they understood the full ramifications of what had happened with their transport, extreme measures had to be taken.

He had spent only fifteen seconds on the phone with Holloway. Though he trusted the man implicitly, that didn't mean someone else wasn't monitoring his calls. Holloway was aware they had escaped the ambush and were presently safe and unharmed.

While Ali had showered, he had poured a bag of rice into a bowl and stuffed his phone into the center of it. He'd removed the case hours ago, hoping the phone might dry out and still function. He'd also found some oil to take care of his weapon.

He would know soon enough if the phone was going to work again, he supposed.

Dressed now, he returned to the kitchen, where Ali's attention was glued to the television.

"You okay?" He asked the question because her face was pale, and her arms were hugged around her body.

"I've been watching the news for the past half hour, and there's nothing about what happened to us."

"I'm sure the situation is being kept quiet. The AUSA will not want anyone to know his one and only witness is out of pocket. Of course, Armone's people are aware of the situation, but they have no idea—hopefully—where we are at present."

She tipped her head in understanding. "So this—" she gestured to the television hanging on the wall "—is a good thing."

"A very good thing."

It was nearing four o'clock. He had to make a decision. "This might be a little too close to where things hit the fan. I'd feel more comfortable if we relocated to a hotel closer to Atlanta."

"Are we going to borrow the car in the garage?" She looked skeptical.

"We are. I'll leave a note for the homeowner in case they come home early. He'll be reimbursed. I'll make sure the car is returned when we're finished."

"Works for me." Beggars couldn't be choosers. She would be thankful for however they escaped the trouble on their heels.

"We should borrow a hat. Maybe a scarf for you."

"I'll go upstairs and find what we need."

"I'll make sure everything is squared away down here."

Jax walked through the first floor, ensuring all was as they'd found it. He'd already done this upstairs. He wrote a note to the homeowner and left it by the phone. Since he couldn't be sure who might come in the house between now and tomorrow, he didn't sign his name. No one needed to know they had been here until Ali had testified.

He grabbed a couple more bottles of water from the fridge, mentally adding it to his tab. He removed his cell from the bowl of rice and cleaned up the mess he'd made. He used a paper towel to go over the phone to ensure there was no more moisture clinging to it. So far so good. He pressed the button to boot it up and hoped for the best.

When the logo appeared and the screen flickered to life, he breathed a sigh of relief. He tucked it into his hip pocket. Since his jacket was still sodden, he'd opted to forgo the shoulder holster and carry his weapon in his waistband. To that end, he left his shirt untucked.

They would need to pick up clothes for tomorrow. A big supercenter-type store would be the best for the purposes of staying anonymous. He always carried a prepaid credit card with him for moments like this. He would use it at the hotel.

Ali descended the stairs. She'd used a scarf to pull her blond hair back. The way the fabric wrapped around her head, her hair was almost completely covered. She handed him a ball cap with the Bulldogs' logo.

"Thanks." He gave her a nod of approval. "Good job on disguising your hair."

"I'm hoping there are sunglasses in the car."

"We're ready then." He settled the hat into place.

Once they were in the garage, he locked the door leading to the house. Ali settled into the passenger seat and fastened her seat belt. He pulled on his own, as well. She checked the glove box and then the console.

"Aha. Sunglasses for everyone." She passed him a pair and slid her own into place.

He tucked the sleek-looking pair she'd given him onto his face. "Nothing like traveling incognito."

They stared at each other for a long moment. He didn't have to see her eyes behind the dark eyewear. She was afraid. She should be. But he would do all within his power to keep her safe.

"Let's do this."

He hit the garage opener and waited while the door slowly slid upward.

Then he backed from the garage, tapped the button again to close the door and then eased out onto the street.

Dusk had fallen, but it wasn't quite dark enough to give him any extra confidence. All they had to do was roll through the neighborhood without drawing any attention and without running into trouble.

ALI REMINDED HERSELF to breathe. Every person on the street seemed to be staring at her as they drove past. But she understood it was her imagination. Other cars glided slowly along the street. Residents coming home from work, probably. A suffocating mixture of worry and fear enveloped her as they met each vehicle.

Would this be the one carrying the bad guys?

How many were searching for them now?

Could they possibly hope to survive the night?

Another turn and they were on the main road, Highway 92, moving away from the neighborhood. The suffocating sensation seeped away. She relaxed against the seat and drew in a big breath. The first hurdle was behind them. Now all they had to do was find a decent motel or hotel close enough to the courthouse but still off the beaten path.

Someplace no one would expect to find them.

As they drove across town, traffic was murder. Their timing couldn't have been worse. Commuters were leaving work, heading home, and everyone wanted to get there first. Patience was less than zero, and aggression was over the top. Ali couldn't help scanning the faces in the cars jammed beside them, in front of them and behind them.

Her nerves were strumming, her ability to breathe constricted again. She recognized the symptoms. She was barreling toward a panic attack. She'd only ever had a few, but she remembered each one distinctly.

It was the most awful feeling. A sensation of being utterly out of control with an overwhelming sense of doom.

"Breathe slow and deep, Ali."

His voice was low and soft, comforting. She would love for him to take the next exit and pull over somewhere so she could get out of this stolen car and run around in circles. Anything to work off the excess adrenaline rushing through her veins.

She struggled to do as he said. Slow, deep, deep, deeper breath. Hold it, let it out slowly. She closed her eyes. Could not analyze another face. This was enough. Enough. It wasn't like they could escape if a car pulled up beside them and the driver or a passenger pointed a weapon at them. There was no place to go in this bumper-to-bumper traffic.

Another slow, deep breath.

Then another.

"We're almost there," he said, the deep resonance of his voice softening the sharp edges of her anxiety.

He took an exit.

Thank God.

She leaned forward and noted the street was North Avenue. He merged into traffic on North and headed east. Then another turn onto North Highland. Traffic wasn't so bad here.

Another slow, steady breath.

A final turn into the parking lot of an inn. He chose a slot far away from the street and shaded by a group of trees and shrubs.

"When we go inside," he said, "I want you to go into the ladies' room. There will be one somewhere close to the lobby. I'll follow you there and ensure there's no one inside. Go into a stall and lock yourself in. When I have a room key, I'll knock on the door and say 'home free.'"

"Okay."

He stared into her eyes, his showing more worry than she suspected he wanted to. "I don't want you standing in front of that counter for the amount of time it will take to get checked in. Plus, it's better if I check in alone. They'll be looking for a couple. Later, we'll go someplace and find clothes for tomorrow. We need to wait until it's quieter on the streets."

"I understand."

He leaned across the console and kissed her forehead. "You're doing great. This has been tough, and you've hung in there every step of the way."

She managed a smile. "Thanks."

Jax scanned the parking lot as they moved toward the side entrance to the lobby. No need to go through the main entrance since they had no luggage and didn't need the assistance of a bellman. Two guests were at the counter checking in, so the clerks paid no attention to them crossing the lobby.

The restrooms were only a few feet down the corridor beyond the registration desk. Directly across from the bank of elevators. He waited at the open door while she checked to ensure no one was in the ladies' room.

"It's clear."

"Lock yourself in a stall, and I'll be back as quickly as possible."

The door closed with a swoosh, and she inspected the four stalls, deciding on the one at the end. She slid the lock into its slot and closed the toilet lid. She sat down and pulled her knees to her chest. If someone came in, maybe they would think this stall was out of order.

The crack in the door was quite narrow, but if anyone really looked they would see her in here.

Hopefully that wouldn't happen. Jax wouldn't be gone that long.

She pressed her chin to her knees and struggled to relax. It was almost over. This time tomorrow she would be out of Atlanta. The AUSA had promised that as soon as she had testified and been cross-examined, she was free to go.

The hydraulic whoosh of the door opening had her head going up. There had been no knock. No code word.

A distinct click, drag and shuffle vibrated in the air.

Ali held her breath. Didn't dare breathe.

A stall door banged inward.

Click. Drag. Shuffle.

Then another door banged inward.

Why didn't the woman pick a stall already?

Unless it wasn't a woman looking for a stall.

The urge to lean down and look beneath the stall wall was overwhelming, but the act would be impossible without dropping her feet to the floor.

The third stall door banged inward. Then another *click.*

Ali's gaze glued to the floor and the metal legs of something beyond her stall door...and white leather shoes...

A sharp rap sounded on the door. "I see you in there."

Ali's heart thundered. She blinked. Her gaze slid around the stall. Stainless steel safety bar. The door had opened outward rather than inward.

Oh hell. She was in the handicap-accessible stall.

"Sorry. I... I'm finished."

Ali slid the lock back and cracked open the door. An elderly lady glared at her as she backed up a step with a click and a drag of her walker and a shuffle of her rubber-soled shoes.

"I'm sorry." Ali slid through the partially opened door. "I was upset and not paying attention."

Thin gray eyebrows arched high on her wrinkled forehead. "I hope you flushed the toilet."

A solid knock on the door followed by, "Home free," saved her from an explanation.

"I did. Sorry."

Ali rushed to the door, pushed it open enough to see Jax and practically fell into his arms.

"You okay?"

"I am now."

THEY ORDERED ROOM service and devoured the food. Somehow, despite the near panic attack she'd had, Ali dozed off on the ultra-soft king-size bed. She hadn't intended to fall asleep, but she'd crawled onto the down comforter and snuggled into the mound of pillows to wait for Jax to say they were ready, and just like that, she was out.

When she opened her eyes again, it was almost eight. She bolted upright.

"Why didn't you wake me?"

He grinned. "You were exhausted. I didn't want to disturb you. You have a big day tomorrow."

Like she could forget.

She scooted off the bed and hurried to the bathroom. She relieved herself and finger-combed her hair. She was a mess. She desperately needed a hairbrush and a toothbrush.

When she'd made herself as presentable as possible, she rejoined Jax, who waited at the door.

"Let's go pick up some clothes."

"I'm as ready as I'll ever be."

He checked the security viewfinder and then

opened the door. "The stairs are on this end of the corridor. They'll take us down to that side door."

Obviously he had done some exploring or research of some sort. The car was parked near that entrance, which would making escaping without being seen far easier.

"Do you know where we're going?" She knew of several supercenters within a twenty-minute drive. She doubted one was any better than the other.

"The closest place and then back here to hole up for the night."

Every moment they were out in the open, the more danger they faced.

"Have you spoken to Holloway or anyone?"

"I called him on my cell." He glanced at her. "It works, but not very well. I managed to get across to him that we would be at the courthouse on time in the morning.

"He said something about an arrest, but I didn't catch all of it. Too much static. I'm assuming that means whoever leaked information about our whereabouts has been found."

"That's good news."

"Holloway is reporting directly to AUSA Knowles, who passes info along to Keller. But he doesn't have our location. No one does. Not even Holloway."

"We should be safe, then," she said, hopeful.

"We should be, yes."

Until tomorrow, when they had to walk into that courthouse.

At the supercenter, they moved quickly through the aisles. Toiletries and other essentials were first on Ali's agenda. Jax grabbed a razor and toiletries of his own. She kind of liked his shadowed jaw. He hadn't shaved since yesterday morning. It was sexy.

"Why are you smiling?" He nodded to the shampoo she held. "You imagining how luscious it will make your hair feel?"

She shook her head, glanced at his chin. "No. Just thinking how much I like this scruffy look."

He rubbed his hand over his jaw. "I'll keep that in mind."

His grin told her he was flattered. She liked his smile. Always had.

"Clothes," he said.

"Right."

The store was more known for its casual wear than for courtroom apparel, but she found a dress that would work. A sweater and shoes plus undergarments and she was good to go.

Jax selected a pair of trousers and a button-down shirt. Socks, shoes and underwear. On second thought he grabbed a belt, too.

Ali's nerves were jittery until they had paid for their merchandise and made their way back to the borrowed car. She liked to think it was *borrowed* rather than stolen.

She hoped none of this came back to haunt Jax.

If his helping her jeopardized his career somehow, she would be devastated.

Driving back to the inn, he asked, "Are you feeling calmer now?"

"Yes. I am. I feel we've made our way over the biggest obstacles and we can see the light at the end of the tunnel."

"We'll get through this," he promised.

The same parking slot was available when they reached the inn. He backed into the space so the license plate wouldn't be visible to anyone cruising through the lot. They hurried inside and up the stairs. Once they were in the room and Jax had done a thorough search, Ali relaxed.

"You hungry? Room service ends in about an hour. Speak now or you're out of luck."

She grabbed the room service menu and perused the offerings. "Cheeseburger, fries and a soft drink."

He made the call and ordered the same as her. While they waited, they hung up tomorrow's wardrobe, content to let the silence settle between them. She thought of all they had been through this day, and she couldn't repress a shudder.

"Jax."

He turned to her, his expression expectant.

"I want you to know that no matter what happens tomorrow, I am very grateful for all you and Marshal Holloway have done." She took a big breath. "I'm not sure I can adequately articulate what it means to me to have had the past few days with you. I never imagined we'd find each other again." She smiled. "Whatever tomorrow brings, this time with you means the world to me."

He pulled her into a kiss. He said everything she wanted to know with his mouth and hands and then with his body.

Chapter Fifteen

Trial day

Thursday, February 6

"There are four FBI agents, four marshals besides me and a good number of Fulton County deputies watching everyone who enters the building."

Jax waited for her to catch up with all that he was saying.

Ali looked worried. Worried and scared and yet strong and brave somehow. However terrified she was, she was damned determined to get this done. He was so proud of her.

But he didn't want to lose her. If there had been any questions whatsoever, those doubts and uncertainties had vanished last night. He had held her against his body and he'd known that she was the part of his life that had been missing all these years. He hadn't wanted a long-term relationship with anyone else because his heart had always belonged to Ali.

"Do you have a route planned out?" she asked as she stared at the map of downtown Atlanta he had spread across the desk.

"We're not taking any direct routes." He pointed to the map. "We'll take North Highland all the way down to Irwin. Then we'll zigzag around and head up to Ivan Allen before dropping down to where we need to be."

"Where will we park?"

"We'll do the same thing we did in Nashville. Park at some church a few blocks away and call for a driver to take us to the front entrance. Sheriff's deputies will come out of the woodwork when I give the signal and form a line on either side of the entrance so no one can get to you from the street between exiting the car and gaining entrance."

"What about some shooter who might be in a neighboring building? Taking aim from some window?" She shook her head. "I've probably seen far too many movies, but when I think of how vicious and ruthless Armone is, I know he's capable of anything."

"We have that covered. Before we so much as step out of the vehicle, the deputies will cover and surround us, ushering us into the building. Making that shot will be virtually impossible. Inside, the marshals will take over and get us to the courtroom."

Ali moistened her lips. "Sounds like a good plan."

"We are prepared to react to anything that occurs."

"What about a bomb?" She tugged at the neck of

the new dress. It was a floral print, and she looked so young and innocent in it.

"Bomb squad is standing by. AUSA Keller isn't taking any chances."

She turned to him. He let her look her fill without saying anything. The cheap trousers, shirt and tie would do. The jacket would work to cover his weapon. The clothes were far from spectacular. Yet she stared at him as if he were some celebrity dressed in a thousand-dollar getup.

"You'll be in the courtroom?"

He smiled. "I will. Security is on high alert. No one is getting into that building with a weapon unless he's a marshal, FBI agent or sheriff's deputy."

It was going to be a long day. Her testimony would take hours, and then there was the cross-examination. As soon as the judge dismissed her, Jax was getting her out of there.

They had made their plan last night. He had already scheduled a few days to visit his parents, but he'd put that off for this assignment. He wanted to take her to Seattle this very evening. She had agreed.

No one was going to stop him.

She had been worried about clothes. He had laughed and said he would buy her a whole new wardrobe.

He held out his hand. "We should get going. You ready?"

"I'm ready."

He'd already done the in-room checkout, so there

was no reason to stop at the registration desk. They exited via the stairwell again. The parking lot was clear. They were in the car and exiting the lot in under three minutes.

The route he'd mapped out went off without a hitch. He found a church at which to park and made the call for an Uber pickup.

Ali grew more nervous with each passing moment. She couldn't keep her hands still. Her eyes roved the parking lot.

"I was thinking," he said, drawing her attention to him. "My apartment is kind of small, and they don't allow pets."

Her gaze widened at the idea that Bob wouldn't be allowed at his place.

"Once we've spent a couple of days with the family, we should probably look for a house. Something with a yard for Bob."

Her lips spread into a smile, and the sheer joy in her eyes affected the rhythm of his heart. "Are you sure that's what you want to do?"

"I am absolutely certain," he confirmed. "I want us to start our new life right away. No more waiting. No putting anything off. Life is too short and too precious."

She stretched across the console and kissed his lips. "I want you to promise me something."

Her face had gone completely serious now.

"Name it." Anything she wanted, if he had the power to make it happen, he intended to.

"Promise me that if you suddenly realize that you've made the wrong decision—" He opened his mouth to argue, but she stopped him with her fingers. "If you've made this decision out of some sense of guilt and you come to realize that going back to what we had before is not what you really want, swear to me that you'll tell me. I don't want you spending your life trying to make up for a decision you made at twenty-two."

"You have my word," he said instead of countering. "If I decide for some reason that I don't want to spend the rest of my life with you or that I don't want you to be my wife and have children with me, then I'll let you know."

She blinked, startled. "What did you say?"

"Which part?" He might be enjoying this a little too much.

"The part in the middle just before the mention of children."

"I want you to marry me, Ali. Tonight, tomorrow, next week, whenever is good for you."

She threw her arms around him, and they hugged. "I love you," he whispered against her hair. "I have for more than a decade."

Ali drew back and looked into his eyes. "I love you, too."

He swept a strand of hair from her cheek. Before he could say more, he spotted the car he was expecting. The driver matched the photo he'd been sent.

"Here's our ride."

He climbed out and walked around to her door. When she emerged, she took his hand and said, "Don't get shot, okay?"

He grinned. "You got it."

THE CAR PULLED to the curb in front of the entrance to the federal building. Ali's heart was pounding so heart she could scarcely breathe.

Immediately a line of uniforms formed on either side of the car door from which they would emerge.

"Ready?"

She nodded.

As the car door opened, something large and black like some sort of tarp was stretched out overhead. Jax climbed out of the car and reached for her hand. She joined him on the sidewalk. As planned, the uniforms closed in around them. She and Jax hunkered down and moved with the mass of uniforms through the doors.

Once they were inside, she managed a breath. The other marshals took over from there, surrounding them and ushering them toward the elevator.

They stepped into the car, and Ali struggled to hold back a looming panic attack. She would not let this happen. Not now. What she was about to do was one of the most important steps in her life. She would not fail.

She and Jax were sequestered in a private room until it was time for her to enter the courtroom.

There hadn't been time to don bulletproof vests. At this point it was no longer necessary. They were inside, well guarded, and anyone who stepped into that courtroom would be, as well.

A few minutes later, she was escorted to the courtroom, Jax at her side. Silence fell over the room as she walked to the witness box. Jax sat behind the AUSA. She stood facing the courtroom, and her gaze immediately lit on Harrison Armone Sr. She stared at him, unflinching. He was surrounded by a team of attorneys, but they would not win. Not this time.

While her former father-in-law stared at her, she took the oath to tell the truth and nothing but the truth. She sat down, and as she did, she smiled at him. She wanted him to know how very much she intended to enjoy this day.

MORNING HAD GIVEN way to late afternoon by the time Ali was finished. They had taken a lunch break and she'd spent that time in the private room with Jax. She hadn't been able to eat. She wasn't sure she could again until she was far away from here.

When she was dismissed, she was escorted out of the courtroom just as she had been when she entered.

Another few minutes were required for her and Jax to be whisked away from the courthouse via a route where they wouldn't be trapped by reporters. Jax had turned over the keys to the borrowed car and given one of the other marshals a list of items owed to the owner.

To Ali's surprise, Marshal Holloway and his friend Chief Brannigan showed up to drive them to the airport.

"You're looking far better," she said to Holloway.

"I don't feel as much like death, that's for sure," he said with a laugh.

She hugged him gently and thanked him again for all he'd done to keep her safe for six long months. He promised to see that Bob arrived safely in Seattle in a couple of weeks. Jax hadn't told her until they were out of the courthouse that he'd already put in for a transfer back to Seattle. He would be on vacation until the transfer was approved.

Two and a half hours later, she and Jax were sitting in first-class seats headed to Seattle.

"I'm thinking," she said, "we should take a honeymoon." She was feeling bold after a lovely cocktail.

Jax chuckled. "Don't you think we should get married first?"

She leaned her head against his shoulder. "Maybe we'll just do it simultaneously. You know, go to some exotic place and get married there."

"We could," he agreed. "But then we'd have to face the wrath of my mother and my sister. They've been waiting for this wedding for a long time."

Ali laughed so hard she lost her breath. "Usually that would be the bride's line."

He pressed his forehead to hers. "We'll do whatever you want to do, Ali. As long as you say, 'I do.'"

"Well, I can do that right now, Marshal. I *so* do." She sealed that promise with a kiss.

* * * * *

Read on for an excerpt of
The Darkness We Hide,
Debra Webb's next book in the
Undertaker's Daughter series!

RIP

Burton Johnston
May 5, 1940–March 9, 2020

Burton Johnston was born in Winchester, Tennessee, on May 5, 1940. He was a loving husband and a respected public servant. His work with the healing of animals made him one of the most beloved citizens in all of Franklin County. He served as county coroner for four decades. Despite being nearly eighty years old, Burt worked every day. He loved his work and his hometown. He will be greatly missed. Burt was predeceased by his beloved wife, Mildred. He is survived by a sister, Sally Jernigan, of Tullahoma.

The family will receive friends on Thursday, March 12, 6:00 to 8:00 p.m., at the DuPont Funeral Home. The family has requested donations to the Franklin County Animal Shelter in lieu of flowers.

One

Rowan DuPont parked on the southeast side of the downtown square. The county courthouse sat smack in the middle of Winchester with streets forming a grid around it. Shops, including a vintage movie theater, revitalized over the past few years by local artisans, lined the sidewalks. Something Rowan loved most about her hometown were the beautiful old trees that still stood above all else. So often the trees were the first things to go when towns received a facelift. Not in Winchester. The entire square had been refreshed, and the majestic old trees still stood.

This morning the promise of spring was impossible to miss. Blooms and leaves sprouted from every bare limb. This was her favorite time of year. A new beginning. Anything could happen.

Rowan sighed. Funny how being back in Winchester had come to mean so much to her these past several months. As a teenager she couldn't wait to get away from home. Growing up in a funeral home had made her different from the other kids. She was the daughter of the undertaker, a curiosity. At twelve tragedy had struck, and she'd lost her twin sister and her mother within months of each other. The painful events had driven her to the very edge. By the time she finished high school, she was beyond ready for a change of scenery. Despite having spent more than twenty years living in the big city, hiding from the memories of home, and a dozen of those two decades working with Nashville's Metro Police Department—in Homicide, no less—she had been forced to see that there was no running away. No hiding from the secrets of her past.

There were too many secrets, too many lies, to be ignored.

Yet, despite all that had happened the first eighteen years of her life, she was immensely glad to be back home.

If only the most painful part of her time in Nashville—serial killer Julian Addington—hadn't followed her home and wreaked havoc those first months after her return.

Rowan took a breath and emerged from her SUV. The morning air was brisk and fresh. More glimpses of spring's impending arrival showed in pots overflowing with tulips, daffodils and crocuses. Those same early bloomers dotted the landscape beds all around the square. It was a new year, and she was very grateful to have the previous year behind her.

She might not be able to change the past, but she

could forge a different future, and she intended to do exactly that.

Closing the door, she smiled as she thought of the way Billy had winked at her as he'd left this morning. He'd settled that cowboy hat onto his handsome head, flashed that sexy smile and winked, leaving her heart fluttering. Four months ago he'd moved into the funeral home with her. The 150-year-old three-story house didn't feel nearly so lonely now. She and Billy had been friends most of their lives and, in truth, she had been attracted to him since she was thirteen or fourteen. But she'd never expected a romantic relationship to evolve. Billy Brannigan was a hometown hero. The chief of police and probably the most eligible bachelor in all of Franklin County. He could have his pick of any of the single women around town. Rowan hadn't expected to be his choice.

She had always been too work oriented to bother with long-term relationships. Too busy for dating on a regular basis.

Billy had made her want long term. He made her believe anything was possible, even moving beyond her tragic past.

The whole town was speculating on when the wedding invitations would go out. Rowan hadn't even considered the possibility. This place where she and Billy were was comfortable. It felt good. Particularly since fate had given them a break the past four months. No trouble beyond the regular, everyday sort. No calls or notes from Julian. No unexplained bodies turning up. And no serial killers had appeared looking for Rowan.

Life was strangely calm and oddly normal.

She would never say as much to Billy, but it was just a little terrifying. The worry that any day, any moment, the next bad thing would happen stalked her every waking moment. Somehow she managed to keep that worry on the back burner. But it was there, waiting for an opportunity to seep into her present.

"Not today," she said aloud.

Today was important. She and Burt Johnston, the county coroner, had breakfast on Monday mornings. She locked her vehicle and started for the sidewalk. The Corner Diner was a lunch staple in Winchester. Had been since the end of the Great Depression. Attorneys and judges who had court often frequented the place for lunch. Most anyone who was someone in the area could be found at the diner. More deals and gossip happened here than in the mayor's office.

But breakfast with the coroner wasn't the only event that made this day so important.

Today she intended to offer her assistant, Charlotte Kinsley, a promotion and a part ownership in the funeral home. Since there were no more DuPonts—Rowan had no children and couldn't say if that would ever happen—she needed to bring someone into the family business. Someone younger who could carry on the DuPont legacy.

Rowan paused outside the diner. The iron bench that sat beneath the plate-glass window was empty.

Surprise furrowed her brow. Burt usually waited there for her. She surveyed the cars lining the sidewalks as far as the eye could see. No sign of Burt's. He was never late, but there was always a first time. After all, he wasn't exactly a young man anymore.

She sank down onto the bench, dug her cell phone from her bag and sent him a text. She was the one who generally kept him waiting, and he never once complained. She certainly wasn't going to do so. His car was a little on the vintage side, as well. Maybe he had car trouble this morning. Worry gnawed at her. A dead battery or a flat tire. Surely he would have called her.

"Morning, Rowan."

She glanced up, smiling automatically. Lance Kirby, one of the attorneys who was not fortunate enough to have an office on the square. The ones who had been around a lifetime held on to that highly sought-after real estate. The others, like Kirby, waited patiently for someone to retire or to die. Meanwhile they showed up for coffee in this highly visible location bright and early every morning.

"Good morning, Lance."

Kirby was a couple of years older than her. He'd lived in Winchester his entire life other than the years he spent at college and law school. He was divorced and had three kids. He'd asked Rowan out to dinner on several occasions. She hoped he didn't ask again this morning. Coming up with an excuse to turn him down was becoming tedious. Surely he was aware that she and Billy were a couple now.

The idea startled her a little. This was the first time in her life that she was half of a couple in the truest sense of the word.

"If you're waiting for Burt, he's parked around back. Every spot around the square was taken before seven this morning." Kirby reached for the door. "People have come early hoping for a chance to get into the Winters trial. Everyone wants to hear the story on that family."

Rowan had been reading about the trial for weeks in the *Winchester Gazette*. "That explains why I had to circle around for a while before I found a spot." She'd forgotten about the small parking area in the back alley behind the diner. "Thanks for telling me. I was worried he'd stood me up."

Kirby laughed. "I don't think any man still breathing would stand you up, Rowan."

She glanced at her cell phone as if it had vibrated. "Oops. I have to take this."

The instant she set the phone to her ear, Kirby went on inside the diner, the bell over the door jingling to announce his entrance.

Thank goodness.

For appearances' sake, she kept the phone to her ear a half a minute, then put it away. To pass the time, she counted the yellow daffodils brimming in the rock planter built around the tree at the edge of the sidewalk. Those lovely yellow flowers were coming up all around the funeral home, too. Her mother had loved gardening. Maybe her mother had hoped to chase away some of the gloom associated with living in a funeral home.

Somehow her father had managed to keep her mother's extensive gardens alive and thriving for all those years. Since her father's death, Rowan had hired a gardener, because she did not have a green thumb at all. She had killed every plant she'd ever tried to nurture. She was not going to be the one who dropped the ball on the family garden.

She glanced up, then down, the sidewalk. Still no sign of Burt. With a sigh, she pushed to her feet. Maybe he was on the phone, which would explain why he hadn't answered her text. Rather than keep waiting, she cut through the narrow side alley to the small rear parking lot. With his taillights facing the back of the diner, Burt's white sedan was nosed up to the bank that faced North Jefferson Street.

Rowan quickened her pace and walked up to the driver's side of his car. Burt sat behind the steering wheel, staring out the windshield.

For a moment Rowan waited for him to glance over and see her, but he didn't move. Whether it was the lax expression on his face or some deep-rooted instinct, she abruptly understood that he was dead.

She tugged at the door handle. Thankfully it opened. Her heart pounding, she bent down. No matter that her brain was telling her he was already gone, she asked, "Burt, you okay?"

Her fingers went instantly to his carotid artery. Nothing.

Rowan snatched her cell from her bag and called

911. She requested an ambulance and the chief of police, then she laid the phone on the ground and reached into the car and pulled Burt from his seat. She grunted with the effort of stretching him out on the pavement. On her knees next to him, she pressed her ear to his chest. No heartbeat. She held her cheek close to his lips. No breath.

Rowan started CPR.

The voice from the speaker of her cell phone confirmed that the ambulance was en route. She informed the dispatcher that she'd started CPR.

Rowan continued the compressions, her eyes burning with emotion. Burt was her friend. She had been gone from Winchester for a very long time, and he had made her feel as if she'd never left. She did not want him to die. Other than Billy, he was the person she felt closest to.

The voice of logic reminded her that Burt was just two months shy of his eightieth birthday.

She ignored the voice and focused on the chest compressions. "Come on, Burt. Don't you die on me."

Facial color was still good. Skin was still warm. He couldn't have been in this condition for long. Hope attempted to make an appearance. But it was short-lived. Even a few minutes could be too many.

Damn it!

The approaching sirens drove home the realization that this was all too real.

The paramedics hurried across the parking lot and

took over her frantic efforts. Rowan pushed to her feet and backed away, her muscles feeling suddenly weak.

"Hey."

She looked up, and Billy's arms were suddenly around her. She leaned against his shoulder and fought the urge to weep.

Burt didn't respond to the efforts of the paramedics. Dr. Harold Schneider, a local physician who had attended university with Burt, came to the scene and pronounced his old friend dead.

By the time the ambulance and Schneider were gone, Rowan felt drained. This was not the way she had expected this day to go. This was supposed to be a good day.

"I'll have one of my officers take Burt's car home," Billy said. He reached into the driver's side floorboard and retrieved Burt's cell phone. As he did, the screen lit. "Looks like he was typing a text for you." Billy glanced at Rowan.

She moved in next to him and looked at the screen. At the top was the text she had sent to him. He hadn't opened it. Behind that was the text box into which he had been typing. She read the words.

I found something you need to see.

Rowan frowned. "Why didn't he just call or...?"

Her words trailed off. Because he had died before he had the chance to finish.

"Maybe he planned on talking to you over breakfast," Billy offered. "He may have recognized that he was having a heart attack and tried to send you a message."

Rowan shook her head. "If you think you're having a heart attack, why not call 911? Why waste precious seconds sending a text about something unrelated to your potentially impending demise?"

It didn't make sense. Burt dealt with death all the time. He was too smart to do something so foolish.

"Can I keep his phone for a while?" She looked to Billy. "I'd like to go through his calls and messages just to be sure there isn't something else in there I need to know about. I'll be sure to get it to his sister when I'm finished."

Billy shrugged and passed her the phone. "We have no reason to believe foul play was involved. Since I'm certain he wouldn't mind, I don't see why not."

"Thanks." The phone felt like a brick in her hand. As little as half an hour ago, Burt may have been holding it, typing those words to her. Her stomach twisted. What had he wanted to show her? Was it so important that he would put telling her above his own safety? If he hadn't been aware he was dying, why try to send a text when they were about to have breakfast together? He was already at the diner, only steps from her.

This was the downside to having friends. Growing up in a funeral home, one would think she would have gotten used to death. But it was different when it was someone close. This was the part that you never got used to.

"I have to get back to the office," Billy said, regret in his voice. "I can take you home first if you'd like."

She shook her head. "I'll be okay." Breakfast was out of the question. She couldn't eat if her life depended upon it. After his wife passed, Burt had told Rowan many times that he wanted her to take care of his final arrangements when the time came. She would need to go back to the funeral home and pick up the hearse so that she could go to the hospital and take charge of his body. "I have to pick up Burt and take care of him. That's what he wanted."

Billy grimaced. "I figured. You're sure you don't need me to help?"

"Charlotte is working today. She'll want to help." Rowan managed a smile. "Thanks, anyway."

She watched Billy drive away before she headed back through the narrow alley and to the front side of the diner where she'd parked her SUV. It had taken two months for Billy to stop being so overprotective. After what happened just before Halloween with Wanda Henegar and Sue Ellen Thackerson, he'd been determined to keep her under constant surveillance. Finally, she'd convinced him that she was okay to drive around town and to be at the funeral home alone. She was armed, her handgun was in her bag and she was vigilant about paying attention to her surroundings.

Rowan settled into the driver's seat of her SUV and started the engine. After her father's murder last year, she had expected to put helping to solve homicides behind her. She had come home to take over the funeral home. Preparing and burying the dead was the only relationship she had expected to have with death. But her father's murderer, Julian Addington, had had other plans. He had haunted her life, even daring to show up in person. Rowan had shot him. Unfortunately he'd survived.

No. She was glad he had survived. She needed Julian alive. There were answers she still wanted. Perhaps that was why her shot had been so far off that day. As much as she wanted him to pay for all that he had done, she also wanted the whole truth. She was sick to death of the bits and pieces of her mother's history. A million little pieces that Rowan couldn't seem to cobble together in a way that made any kind of sense.

She stared at Burt's cell phone, wishing it held the answers she needed, but of course it did not. Admittedly, she had learned a good deal since returning to Winchester. Her mother had been involved with Julian Addington, currently one of the most prolific serial killers in documented history. The depth of her involvement was unknown. If Anna Addington, Julian's ex-wife, was to be believed, Julian had been obsessed with Norah, Rowan's mother. After her death, he had become obsessed with Rowan— all that was left of her since his own daughter had murdered Rowan's twin sister, Raven.

If all that wasn't complicated enough, Norah

DuPont appeared to have had many friends besides Julian who were killers. Like the one who had curated the faces and skin of his victims—all of whom turned out to be serial killers who were never caught. The FBI had had them labeled as inactive. Finding those faces had solved hundreds of cases.

There was even some circumstantial evidence that Rowan's father, Edward, was involved on some level. Julian would have Rowan believe that Edward had killed Julian's daughter, Alisha, after she murdered Raven. But Rowan refused to believe such nonsense. Her father had not been capable of murder. She would never believe otherwise.

But finding the truth she sought was not easy. Her parents were dead. Herman Carter, her father's lifelong friend and assistant at the funeral home, was dead. He'd committed suicide after Rowan discovered his treachery—the black marketing of stolen body parts. It seemed the harder she searched for accurate information, the taller the brick walls and the murkier the pictures she discovered.

Her mother had been a loner—at least, that was what everyone had always thought. She'd traveled frequently doing research for her writing. Norah DuPont had been a self-proclaimed writer. She'd had no friends—at least, no real ones that Rowan had found. Her father's one good friend was dead.

Rowan certainly couldn't trust anything Julian told her.

As grateful as she was for the past few months of

peace and quiet, the uneventful period also worried her. What was Julian up to? It was possible he was dead, she supposed. The consensus of most involved with the investigation was that she had only winged him. But he had not been spotted since she shot him in May of last year. She had heard from him a couple of times but nothing since last fall.

If he was alive, he was no doubt readying for some sort of strike. Lining up all his ducks, as they say. But last October another facet had been added to this strange situation. A man whose name she did not know had appeared to help her out of a deadly situation. He had claimed her mother sent him to protect her.

But her mother was dead. Had been for almost twenty-eight years.

Rowan shook her head. Just when she thought she had cleared up one aspect of this insanity, two more things cropped up, adding additional questions and leading her in a whole new and bizarre direction.

She stared at Burt's phone. Touched the Home key to awaken the screen. Luckily he had no pass code. She checked his text messages and his call log. She even reviewed his emails. Nothing except veterinary and coroner talk. Conferences. New cutting-edge drug therapies.

Nothing about her or her family or Julian.

"What in the world did you need to show me, Burt?"

A sharp rap on her window made her practically jump out of her skin. Her heart in her throat, she lifted her gaze to the figure hovering only inches from the glass.

Lance Kirby.

She dragged in a breath as she powered down her window. Somehow she produced a smile for the persistent man. "Sorry. I was a thousand miles away."

Actually, she'd only been a few, but he had no need to know that.

"I didn't mean to startle you." He reached through the window, squeezed her shoulder, his fingers lingering a little longer than necessary. "I just wanted to say how sorry I am. I heard about Burt." He jerked his head toward the diner. "It's a shame. A real shame."

Rowan nodded. "It is. He'll be missed."

Kirby launched into a list of all the ways he would be happy to help in whatever way she needed. Rowan finally found an opening in his monologue and explained that she had to go pick up Burt.

Kirby managed a strained smile and said he understood. He stepped back and stood on the sidewalk watching as she drove away.

She probably should feel bad for blowing him off, but she didn't.

The only thing on her mind right now was taking care of Burt.

Two

Burt had been a tall man. A little better than six feet. Like many, he had put on some extra weight as he grew older; his thicker abdomen warned of how much he had loved sweets. Charlotte had helped Rowan handle moving the body. Now Burt was undressed and positioned on the mortuary table, his head stationed on the head block.

His longtime friend and personal physician, Harold Schneider, had come by and examined the body. With Burt's recently diagnosed heart condition, a sudden heart attack was common. Dr. Schneider took care of the necessary paperwork for the death certificate. Since there was no indication of foul play and in light of Burt's advanced age and recent medical history, there was no need for an autopsy.

His body had been washed, disinfected and moisturized. Rigor mortis had invaded his limbs. Rowan had massaged them to help loosen up the muscles. Lividity had set in along the backs of his arms and his torso but more prominently in his buttocks and the backs of the thighs, since he had been in a seated position when his heart first stopped beating. Moving him so quickly after death had shifted the lividity to some degree, but the discoloration remained in the initially affected areas.

No matter that both rigor and lividity were present, Rowan checked his corneas, finding them cloudy, and then his carotid pulse, which was no longer present. This final examination before beginning the no-turning-back steps was a part of the process she never ignored. Her father had told her a few startling stories passed down from his father and grandfather about undertakers making incisions for the pump lines only to discover the heart was still beating, sending blood spewing. Better to take every precaution first.

After making the necessary incisions in the preferred arteries, she inserted the tubes for draining the body fluids and replacing them with the preserving chemicals used in the embalming process. The process required approximately forty-five minutes.

The sound of the pump churning filled the room. The sound was as familiar as her own heartbeat. This moment was certainly the end of an era. First, her father had died, then Herman and now Burt. The three had been in the business of taking care of the dead in this town for half a century or more.

With a sigh, Rowan removed her gloves, mask and apron. She set them aside for when she returned and went upstairs to find Charlotte. There hadn't been time to talk after she arrived back at the funeral home with Burt. As sadly as this morning had started, Rowan wanted to move forward with her plan.

She found Charlotte in her office already laying out the design for Burt's memorial pamphlet. Rowan paused behind her chair and studied the image on the screen.

"That's a great photo of Burt." He looked like the jolly man everyone had known him to be. "The layout is nice. Burt would be honored."

"Thank you. I wanted to do this in a way that I knew he would like. I found the photo in all those pics we took at the dinner you hosted at Christmas."

Rowan smiled at the memory. Burt's wife had died only a month before, and his sister was on a holiday cruise that had been planned for nearly a year. Rowan had insisted Burt come to her dinner. She had invited her staff, including the cleaning team. By the day of the party, it had turned into such a large gathering she'd held it in the lobby instead of in her kitchen in the living quarters.

"That was a great party," Rowan said, mostly to herself.

"It sure was," Charlotte agreed. She glanced over her shoulder. "You know you'll have to do that every year from now on."

Not in a million years would she have ever thought she would be hosting parties in this funeral home. But Charlotte was right. It needed to become a tradition. Their work was so somber, infusing happiness wherever possible was important. Rowan took a breath. It was time she started a number of new traditions. This was her home, her business now. She was no longer just the undertaker's daughter; she was the undertaker. There were many things she could do.

Rowan pulled up a chair. "Do you have a few minutes to talk?"

Charlotte spun her chair to face Rowan. Worry darkened her expression. "Of course. Is everything okay?"

Rowan nodded. "Other than Burt's sudden death, yes, everything is great."

That voice, the one that whispered to her far too frequently, reminding her that the other shoe could drop at any moment, nagged at her, but Rowan ignored it.

"I'm the last DuPont," Rowan announced. "There's no one else."

Charlotte gave her a look over the top of her computer glasses. "You and Billy are getting married and having babies. There will be plenty of DuPont-Brannigans."

Rowan laughed. She couldn't help herself. "I appreciate your optimism, Charlotte, but I hit the big four-oh recently. I'm not holding my breath. Besides, there has been no proposal from the other half of your equation." She cocked her head and studied her assistant. "Unless you know something I don't."

Frankly, Rowan wasn't sure she was ready for that step for numerous reasons. She and Billy had been best friends for so long the idea of doing anything that might damage that relationship was terrifying. She'd struggled with that fear when they decided to take their relationship to the next level. The idea of getting married—a lifetime commitment—was truly frightening. What kind of wife would she be? Good grief, what kind of mother would she be when she had only Norah for an example?

Charlotte held up her hands. "I do not know anything. I'm just saying."

Rowan waved her off. "Anyway, I'm having my attorney draw up a contract."

A frown marred the other woman's face.

"I'm giving you a promotion along with a substantial raise." She named the figure, and Charlotte's jaw dropped. Before she could voice a protest, Rowan went on. "I'm also going to add a bonus of 5 percent interest in the funeral home starting this year and 1 percent each year of service moving forward—as long as the profit margins remain stable or rising."

"Oh no. You can't do that! The very idea is far too generous, Rowan. The salary increase alone is more than enough."

"Trust me," Rowan argued, "this is a better deal for me than for you."

The younger woman pressed a hand to her chest. "I'm so flattered and grateful. I don't know what to say." She blinked against the emotion shining in her eyes. "I can't tell you how much this means to me. I love working with you, and I love the job." She laughed. "I know it sounds strange, but I enjoy working with the dead and their families. I feel like it's very important work."

Rowan smiled. "This is why you're a perfect partner."

Charlotte swiped at her eyes, her lips trembling with the effort of holding a smile in place. "Thank you."

"When the attorney has the agreement drafted, we'll have him bring it here for signature and then we'll have another party." Rowan stood. "I should go check on Burt."

Charlotte thanked her again before she could get out the door. The reaction was what Rowan had hoped for and certainly bolstered her low mood. She headed back along the hall and down the stairs to the basement and on to the mortuary room. There was an elevator for transporting gurneys and coffins from floor to floor, but she only used it when she was moving a client.

Freud, her German shepherd, was stretched out on the floor in the corridor just outside the mortuary room door. He lifted his head from his paws as she approached. The mortuary room was off-limits to Freud, but she had a feeling he understood that their friend Burt was in there.

"Hey, boy." She scratched the top of his head. "You missing our buddy, too?"

Freud and Rowan had much in common; they both had painful pasts. The first three years of his life had been spent being kicked around and neglected by his drug-trafficking owner. Rowan had found him when she and her team from the Nashville Metro Police Department were investigating a man who had murdered at least four people. As soon as the scum-bag was arrested, Rowan went back for Freud. Of course, she hadn't known his name. The dog hadn't been registered. He hadn't ever been to a vet. She made sure he had everything he needed, including a complete checkup, and he was answering to the name Freud in no time.

They had been good for each other. They had both survived their broken pasts and learned to trust again.

"Come on, boy. We'll make an exception today. You can join me in the mortuary room."

Freud followed her to the stainless-steel table where Burt waited and stretched out on the cool tile floor. Rowan checked the pump's progress. Another five minutes and the task would be complete. She donned her apron, mask and gloves once more. After she removed the tubes and pushed the pump aside, she closed the incisions she had made.

A few more minutes were required to check the rest of her work. His face was set. Jaw wired shut. Lips and eyes sealed. The nose and other orifices had been cleaned and packed to ensure no leakages. Since his wake and funeral wouldn't be for a few days, she would wait about adding any topical cosmetics.

She rolled the gurney next to the mortuary table, applied the brakes and transferred Burt onto it. She adjusted the sheet covering his private areas and added another larger sheet that would cover him fully. For now, she would park him in refrigeration until time for his service. His sister was trying to get an earlier flight from Cozumel. She hadn't planned to return until this weekend. Under the circumstances, she hoped to be back by Thursday. Burt's viewing—wake or visitation, as many called it—was tentatively scheduled for Thursday. All Rowan needed at this point was some direction on the clothing his sister wanted her to use. She was supposed to call with an update.

"See you tomorrow, Burt."

Rowan exited the refrigeration unit and locked the door. Since a body had been stolen last October, she had started locking the unit door. That likely wouldn't stop anyone determined enough to force his way into the funeral home, but with the security system it made getting in and then out far more difficult to accomplish in the scarce few minutes between the alarm going off and the police arriving.

Her stomach rumbled, and she reminded herself that she hadn't eaten today. Breakfast had been long forgotten, and then she'd needed to take care of Burt. It was almost noon, and this was the first time she'd thought of food.

Freud followed her into the lobby. The front entry to the funeral home was fairly grand. Folks expected it to be. The lobby was spacious with clusters of seating areas. Charlotte ensured the many plants adorning the spacious area were watered and pruned as necessary. Lots of windows allowed the light to pour in during the day. At night the blinds behind the heavy drapes provided privacy and a sense of coziness. The shiny floors were blanketed with muted Persian rugs that were nearly as old as the funeral home itself. If she were to continue beyond the lobby, there was a corridor that led to a refreshment lounge, her office and the public restrooms. In the other direction were the viewing parlors and the chapel. Directly across from the main entrance and set back to ensure it was visible as a backdrop to all else stood the grand staircase that ascended up to the second floor.

Rowan stood at the newel post, looking upward as she often did. The wide stairs were lined with a Persian runner. The stairs rose up and spilled onto the landing. The ornate railing stood beneath the massive chandelier that lit not only the lower but also the upper level, as well. Beyond the chandelier was the towering stained-glass window depicting angels ascending to heaven. When Rowan was a child, her mother had painstakingly restored the beautiful stained glass.

But that had been before.

Before she tied a rope to that ornate banister and hanged herself. Just in time for her only surviving daughter to walk through the front entrance and find her. The police had come, and when they had finished documenting the scene, her father had been allowed to pull her mother over that railing and cut her loose. He had held her in his arms and cried like a baby.

Rowan couldn't climb these stairs without thinking of how her own mother had betrayed her, which was why she more often than not used the back staircase. But sometimes these stairs were just handier.

Besides, if she faced that hurtful part of her past often enough, perhaps she would grow immune to the pain.

Next to her, Freud whimpered.

"Come on, boy." Rowan started the climb, and Freud followed.

Before everything happened—before her closest friend and mentor, Julian Addington, had been revealed as a serial killer—Rowan had come to terms to some degree with what her mother had done. Since she had hanged herself only months after Raven drowned, Rowan had always assumed that her mother had loved her dead daughter too much to go on without her. Too much to grin and bear life for her remaining daughter.

During the past year, Rowan had discovered many secrets about her mother. Not the least of which was that she had likely blamed herself for Raven's death, which might explain why she couldn't live with what happened.

Still, she had left Rowan as a twelve-year-old child to grow up believing her mother hadn't loved her enough to stay. But Rowan had had her father. He had always been the perfect parent. Loving, patient, kind.

Sadly, he had been keeping secrets, too.

So very many secrets had been buried, and so many lies had been told. So much darkness to find her way through.

It was difficult to distinguish what was fact from what was fiction.

At the top of the stairs, she made the right into the corridor that led to the living quarters. The second floor and the smaller third floor had served as the family home for several generations of DuPonts. When the funeral home was built a century and a half ago, that had been the plan. All these years later, that reality had not changed.

Rowan unlocked the door that separated her private space from the public funeral home space. This was new, as well. Billy had insisted she have as many security barriers as possible between her and any trouble that found her.

She smiled as she opened the door. Now she had Billy, too.

On Halloween night last fall, she had invited him to stay with her. It was the first time they were together in that way. She closed the door behind Freud and moved on to the kitchen. She opened the fridge door and scanned the contents.

Being with Billy was exactly as she had imagined. Amazing. Beautiful. Perfect.

At first she had been terrified. What if things went wrong and her and Billy's friendship was damaged by the falling apart of their physical entanglement?

So far that had not happened. Shortly after that first time together, he had moved in. They shared the same room she had slept in her whole life before going off to college. They had talked about cleaning out the larger bedroom that had belonged to her parents, but until all these mysteries were solved, she just didn't want to tackle the job. It felt as if she needed everything to stay just as it had always been.

Besides, for now they were taking things one step at a time. No rushing. No stress. Just enjoying this new aspect of their relationship.

She grabbed the bologna and mustard—one of Billy's go-to snacks—and made a sandwich. When she'd filled a glass with water, she gave Freud a snack and went to the table. As she ate she thought about dinner at Billy's parents' house yesterday. Dottie, his mother, had hinted repeatedly at the idea of a wedding. She wanted grandchildren. But first and foremost she wanted her son happy. Dottie understood that Billy wanted to be with Rowan. Dottie was a wonderful mother. She was kind and generous to Rowan, and she would be an amazing grandmother.

But what if things didn't work out?

She was so worried that her relationship with Billy would be over completely if this new closer, more intimate relationship fell apart.

Rowan looked down at Freud, who watched her every move in hopes of getting a bite of her lunch. "It's complicated, boy. It's not easy being human."

She laughed. "It's not easy being a dog, either, huh?" Freud had definitely survived a few complications of his own.

Rowan finished off her sandwich and cleaned up the crumbs. She pushed in her chair and walked to the window that overlooked the backyard. Was she ready for the next steps? Marriage? Children?

She shook her head, reminding herself she hadn't been asked. Dottie and Charlotte were putting foolish ideas in her head.

Her arms went around her waist as another cold, harsh reality invaded her thoughts. There was the ever-present concern about Julian. She couldn't pretend he was gone forever. She could hope, but there was no way to be certain. He would destroy Billy just to get at her. The serial killer Angel Petrov, who had showed up at the funeral home with a body in her suitcase, had warned Rowan that Billy might not be long for this world.

He has a very large target on his back.

Whatever else she did, Rowan had to be sure there was no threat to Billy. Just because there had been no contact from Julian and no other killers had shown up with messages or bodies didn't mean the nightmare was over.

Rowan exhaled a big breath. It might never be truly over.

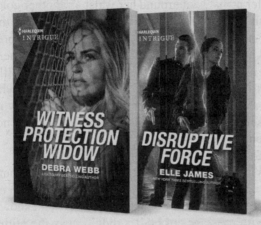

#1911 BEFORE HE VANISHED
A Winchester, Tennessee Thriller • by Debra Webb
Halle Lane's best friend disappeared twenty-five years ago, but when
Liam Hart arrives in Winchester, Halle's certain he's the boy she once knew.
As the pair investigates Liam's mysterious past, can they uncover the truth
before a killer buries all evidence of the boy Halle once loved?

#1912 MYSTERIOUS ABDUCTION
A Badge of Honor Mystery • by Rita Herron
Cora Reeves's baby went missing in a fire five years ago, but she's convinced
the child is still out there. When Sheriff Jacob Maverick takes on the cold
case, new leads begin to appear—as well as new threats.

#1913 UNDERCOVER REBEL
The Mighty McKenzies Series • by Lena Diaz
Homeland Security agent Ian McKenzie has been working undercover
to break up a human-trafficking ring, but when things go sideways,
Shannon Murphy is suddenly caught in the crosshairs. Having only recently
learned the truth about Ian, can Shannon trust him with her life?

#1914 SOUTH DAKOTA SHOWDOWN
A Badlands Cops Novel • by Nicole Helm
Sheriff Jamison Wyatt has spent his life helping his loved ones escape his
father's ruthless gang. Yet when Liza Dean's sister finds herself caught in the
gang's most horrifying crime yet, they'll have to infiltrate the crime syndicate
and find her before it's too late.

#1915 PROTECTIVE OPERATION
A Stealth Novel • by Danica Winters
Shaye Geist and Chad Martin are both hiding from powerful enemies in the
wilds of Montana, and when they find an abandoned baby, they must join
forces. Can they keep themselves and the mysterious child safe—even as
enemies close in on all sides?

#1916 CRIMINAL ALLIANCE
Texas Brothers of Company B • by Angi Morgan
There's an algorithm that could destroy Dallas, and only FBI operative
Therese Ortis and Texas Ranger Wade Hamilton can find and stop it. But
going undercover is always dangerous. Can they accomplish their goal
before they're discovered?

SPECIAL EXCERPT FROM

H HARLEQUIN
INTRIGUE

*Sheriff Jamison Wyatt has never forgotten Liza Dean,
the one who got away. But now she's back, and she needs
his help to find her sister. They'll have to infiltrate a crime
syndicate, but once they're on the inside, will they
be able to get back out?*

Read on for a sneak preview of
South Dakota Showdown *by Nicole Helm.*

Chapter One

Bonesteel, South Dakota, wasn't even a dot on most maps, which
was precisely why Jamison Wyatt enjoyed being its attached
officer. Though he was officially a deputy with the Valiant County
Sheriff's Department, as attached officer his patrol focused on
Bonesteel and its small number of residents.

One of six brothers, he wasn't the only Wyatt who acted as an
officer of the law—but he was the only man who'd signed up for
the job of protecting Bonesteel.

He'd grown up in the dangerous, unforgiving world of a biker
gang run by his father. The Sons of the Badlands were a cutthroat
group who'd been wreaking havoc on the small communities of
South Dakota—just like this one—for decades.

Luckily, Jamison had spent the first five years of his life on his
grandmother's ranch before his mother had fully given in to Ace
Wyatt and moved them into the fold of the nomadic biker gang.

Through tenacity and grit Jamison had held on to a belief in
right and wrong that his grandmother had instilled in him in those
early years. When his mother had given birth to son after son on the
inside of the Sons, Jamison had known he would get them out—
and he had, one by one—and escape to their grandmother's ranch
situated at the very edge of Valiant County.

HIEXP0220

It was Jamison's rough childhood in the gang and the immense responsibility he'd placed on himself to get his brothers away from it that had shaped him into a man who took everything perhaps a shade too seriously. Or so his brothers said.

Jamison had no regrets on that score. Seriousness kept people safe. He was old enough now to enjoy the relative quiet of patrolling a small town like Bonesteel. He had no desire to see lawbreaking. He'd seen enough. But he had a deep, abiding desire to make sure everything was right.

So it was odd to be faced with a clear B and E just a quarter past nine at night on the nearly deserted streets. Maybe if it had been the general store or gas station, he might have understood. But the figure was trying to break into his small office attached to city hall.

It was bold and ridiculous enough to be moderately amusing. Probably a drunk, he thought. Maybe the…woman—yes, it appeared to be a woman—was drunk and looking to sleep it off.

When he did get calls, they were often alcohol related and mostly harmless, as this appeared to be.

Since Jamison was finishing up his normal last patrol for the night, he was on foot. He walked slowly over, keeping his steps light and his body in the shadows. The streets were quiet, having long since been rolled up for the night.

Still, the woman worked on his doorknob. If she was drunk, she was awfully steady for one. Either way, she didn't look to pose much of a threat.

He stepped out of the shadow. "Typically people who break and enter are better at picking a lock."

The woman stopped what she was doing—but she hadn't jumped or shrieked or even stumbled. She just stilled.

Don't miss
South Dakota Showdown *by Nicole Helm,*
available March 2020 wherever
Harlequin Intrigue books and ebooks are sold.

Harlequin.com

Get 4 FREE REWARDS!

We'll send you 2 FREE Books plus 2 FREE Mystery Gifts.

Harlequin Intrigue books are action-packed stories that will keep you on the edge of your seat. Solve the crime and deliver justice at all costs.

FREE Value Over **$20**

YES! Please send me 2 FREE Harlequin Intrigue novels and my 2 FREE gifts (gifts are worth about $10 retail). After receiving them, if I don't wish to receive any more books, I can return the shipping statement marked "cancel." If I don't cancel, I will receive 6 brand-new novels every month and be billed just $4.99 each for the regular-print edition or $5.99 each for the larger-print edition in the U.S., or $5.74 each for the regular-print edition or $6.49 each for the larger-print edition in Canada. That's a savings of at least 12% off the cover price! It's quite a bargain! Shipping and handling is just 50¢ per book in the U.S. and $1.25 per book in Canada.* I understand that accepting the 2 free books and gifts places me under no obligation to buy anything. I can always return a shipment and cancel at any time. The free books and gifts are mine to keep no matter what I decide.

Choose one: ☐ **Harlequin Intrigue Regular-Print** (182/382 HDN GNXC) ☐ **Harlequin Intrigue Larger-Print** (199/399 HDN GNXC)

Name (please print)

Address   Apt. #

City   State/Province   Zip/Postal Code

Mail to the **Reader Service**:
IN U.S.A.: P.O. Box 1341, Buffalo, NY 14240-8531
IN CANADA: P.O. Box 603, Fort Erie, Ontario L2A 5X3

Want to try 2 free books from another series! Call 1-800-873-8635 or visit www.ReaderService.com.

*Terms and prices subject to change without notice. Prices do not include sales taxes, which will be charged (if applicable) based on your state or country of residence. Canadian residents will be charged applicable taxes. Offer not valid in Quebec. This offer is limited to one order per household. Books received may not be as shown. Not valid for current subscribers to Harlequin Intrigue books. All orders subject to approval. Credit or debit balances in a customer's account(s) may be offset by any other outstanding balance owed by or to the customer. Please allow 4 to 6 weeks for delivery. Offer available while quantities last.

Your Privacy—The Reader Service is committed to protecting your privacy. Our Privacy Policy is available online at www.ReaderService.com or upon request from the Reader Service. We make a portion of our mailing list available to reputable third parties that offer products we believe may interest you. If you prefer that we not exchange your name with third parties, or if you wish to clarify or modify your communication preferences, please visit us at www.ReaderService.com/consumerschoice or write to us at Reader Service Preference Service, P.O. Box 9062, Buffalo, NY 14240-9062. Include your complete name and address.

HI20R

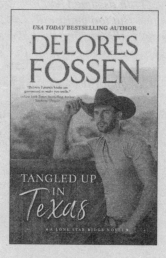

*As teenagers, they couldn't get enough of each other.
So when Sunny Dalton returns to her hometown of Lone
Star Ridge, Texas, and is reunited with Shaw Jameson,
the sparks they both assumed had long fizzled out are
quickly reignited. But too many old secrets lay hidden
below the surface, threatening the happily-ever-after
they've never given up on...*

Read on for a sneak peek at
Tangled Up in Texas,
the first book in Lone Star Ridge from
USA TODAY *bestselling author Delores Fossen.*

Shaw looked up when he heard the sound of the
approaching vehicle. Not coming from behind but rather
ahead—from the direction of the ranch. It was a dark
blue SUV barreling toward him, and it screeched to a
stop on the other side of the intimate apparel he'd found
lying on the road.

Because of the angle of the morning sunlight and the
SUV's tinted windshield, Shaw couldn't see the driver,
but he sure as heck saw the woman who stepped from the
passenger's side.

Talk about a gut punch of surprise. The biggest
surprise of the morning, and that was saying something
considering the weird underwear on the road.

Sunny Dalton.

She was a blast from the past and a tangle of memories. And here she was walking toward him like a siren in her snug jeans and loose gray shirt.

And here he was on the verge of drooling.

Shaw did something about that and made sure he closed his mouth, but he knew it wouldn't stay that way. Even though Sunny and he were no longer teenagers, his body just steamed up whenever he saw her.

Sunny smiled at him. However, he didn't think it was so much from steam but rather a sense of polite frustration.

"Shaw," she said on a rise of breath.

Her voice was smooth and silky. Maybe a little tired, too. Even if Shaw hadn't seen her in a couple of years, he was pretty sure that was fatigue in her steel blue eyes.

She'd changed her hair. It was still a dark chocolate brown, but it no longer hung well past her shoulders. It was shorter in a nonfussy sort of way, which would have maybe looked plain on most women. On Sunny, it just framed that amazing face.

And Shaw knew his life was about to get a whole lot more complicated.

Don't miss
Tangled Up in Texas *by Delores Fossen,*
available March 2020 wherever
HQN Books and ebooks are sold!

HQNBooks.com